GHOSTLY TALES OF THE UNEXPECTED

By

Simon Entwistle

GHOSTLY TALES OF THE UNEXPECTED

Copyright © Simon Entwistle 2014

Published by Simon Entwistle 2014

Simon Entwistle has asserted his right under the Copyright, Designs and Patents Act 1988 to be identified as the author of this work.

This novel is a work of fiction, inspired by traditional folklore. Names and characters are the product of folklore, and the author's own imagination and any resemblance to any persons, living or dead, is entirely coincidental.

This book is sold subject to the condition that it shall not, by way of trade or otherwise, be lent, resold, hired out, or otherwise circulated without the publishers prior consent in any form of binding or cover other than that in which it is published and without a similar condition including this condition being imposed on the subsequent purchaser.

Cover Design by Steven Suttie

Font Type Baskerville Old Face

1st Edition

INTRODUCTION

Ghost stories do seem to fascinate people all over the planet. Everybody has heard the expression "you look like you have just seen a ghost." This subject seems to attract divine attention. I am not a psychic, medium or clairvoyant, but I do believe that there is life after death in a Christian sense.

I am a tour guide running my own business, The vast majority of my tour take in ghosts, murders and mysteries. I am a regular visitor to schools and university lecture halls, and have also presented a series on ITV 1 called "Into The Unknown."

One thing I can always guarantee is a captive audience. This does beat working for a living. My affair with ghost stories started in the summer of 1975. In this year I joined the army and was informed by the recruitment officer in Carlisle that I would see the world. I had no idea that his words would come true on my first day as a recruit.

The army sent me to the Infantry Training School in York. On arriving at the railway station, I was completely taken in by the stunning architecture of the station. At this moment, I suddenly realised that York had a superb atmosphere about it. I climbed into the back of a 3 ton Bedford truck and as the vehicle made its way through the city, my eyes feasted on the awesome minster, Lendal and Skeldergate bridges and Bootham bar. It was love at first sight, I just wanted to climb out of the vehicle and explore. I got to know the city like the back of my hand as a result of going on city tours with excellent guides.

One night I went on a city ghost walk with a truly marvellous York born tour guide called Tony Mercer, who in my view, is the best ghost guide in the city. Tony conducted a tour that sowed a seed in my head. On arrival back home in Clitheroe, Lancashire, I started the Clitheroe Ghost Walks. This book features stories from all of my tours in Lancashire, Yorkshire and Cumbria.

I have thrown a huge amount of fiction into these stories, and mixed them with non-fiction. For instance, The Taxi and The Move are totally fictitious tales that I have written for your entertainment.

These stories are all designed to capture your imagination, and I hope that you enjoy reading them as much as I did writing them.

Special thanks to Patricia Carter and Vic Groves who made the publication of this book possible.

Simon Entwistle

GHOSTLY TALES OF THE UNEXPECTED
Chapter 1

The coach made its way at great speed through the narrow West Riding lanes, the six horses gasping for breath with their eyes staring straight into the twilight. Inside the coach sat Jonty Martindale who was squinting at his timepiece.

"It will soon be dark," he whispered. His thoughts were some 20 miles away in Bromley Cross with his wife, Jane, who was expecting their first child and he had promised her that he would be by her side for the birth.

Suddenly, the village of Whalley came into view and then the Swan Hotel where Jonty could stretch his legs whilst the horses were fed. The horses and the coach came to a halt in the hotel courtyard with the steam and breath from the exhausted horses filling the air. It was bitterly cold outside and Jonty gratefully made his way inside the Swan Hotel. He was greeted by a warm, glowing fire and the landlord, Mr John Nicholson, who recognised him from his previous visits.

"Nice to see you again Jonty. There's a warm meal waiting for you in the back room and a glass of warm punch."

"Thank you Mr. Nicholson," he replied, "When will the horses be ready? I must get back home to my wife because she is expecting our first child and she could go into labour at any time. I must get home tonight!"

"Don't worry Jonty, the horses are just being fed and watered in the stables, so enjoy your meal as they won't be long." replied John Nicholson.

Jonty Martindale was a cotton salesman and his job was to visit the city of Liverpool to buy cotton bales from the Merchant Halls in the city. He was an expert on cotton quality and would take samples from the bales and then use the samples to take orders from the textile barons of Lancashire and Yorkshire. He was well liked and certainly had a very bright future in his chosen profession. His wife, Jane, was extremely proud of him and after two years of marriage, was delighted to conceive and their future together did indeed look very rosy.

Jonty was given a plate of Lancashire hotpot which he consumed at great speed with the glass of punch quickly following. He was the only person on the coach when it arrived, but the Swan Hotel, Whalley, was also a pick-up point for fellow travellers. This winter of 1882 was particularly cold and there had been very serious snowdrifts all over East Lancashire. Jonty gazed out of the warm hotel room through a frosty window just as the snow had started to fall again. He got to his feet and began to pace the room and his fellow guests realised he was somewhat agitated. Jonty nervously looked at his fellow guests and informed them that his wife was expecting their first child and it was imperative he got home that night because she could go into labour at any time. He had also promised her he would be there for the birth and couldn't let her down.

Jonty made his way to the front room of the hotel which faced the main entrance. He looked at his timepiece again and then, as he looked out of the window into the pale moonlight, he noticed a coach waiting outside the hotel. On the coach door he could just make out the words Lancaster and Manchester.

"That's my coach," he muttered excitedly to himself. He ran outside, grabbed the coach door and jumped into the carriage. It felt very damp and musty inside with a not too pleasant aroma. After a few seconds he became aware that he was not alone, as inside the coach, in the hazy pale light, he could make out two still figures both wearing Victorian bonnets which obscured their faces. One was sitting next to him and the other directly opposite with a baby wrapped in blankets on her lap. He tried to get a conversation going as the coach started to move forward.

"It's rather unpleasant in here ladies. Would either of you mind if I opened the window to let in a bit of fresh air?" he requested. There was no answer from either of the ladies and indeed the baby remained rigid as if sleeping soundly. Again Jonty requested the need to open the window and was met by the same silence from both women.

The aroma within the coach became very unpleasant and so Jonty, in a fit of temper, stood up and reached for the leather strap connected to the coach's window frame. To his horror the strap and wooden casing came out in his hand. It was rotten. He then heard a high pitched scream that went through his entire body. He turned and standing next to him was one of the women. She raised her head to look at him and Jonty to his horror suddenly realised that where there should have been a face, there was in fact a hollow cavity. He screamed in terror and kicked open the coach door which splintered easily due to its decayed and rotten condition. He fell out of the coach and his head hit the road surface knocking him unconscious.

The coach carried on into the inky dark night. Some fifteen minutes later Jonty got to his feet nursing a nasty head wound and walked back to Whalley in a blinding blizzard. Exhausted and frozen and suffering from a severe headache, he returned to the Swan Hotel. On entering the hotel, landlord John Nicholson said urgently,

"Mr Martindale, let me dress that head wound. Where have you been to get an injury like this?"

Jonty blurted out in an alarmed voice, "I got in the coach and there was a woman who had no face. The stench in there was overpowering!"

John Nicholson laughed, "Jonty that is impossible! Your coach is still at the back of the hotel and the horses are still being fed and watered. If you would care to look outside, the snow is so deep no coach has left or arrived after yours this afternoon."

Jonty shouted, "I swear to you John, I got in a coach! It was the Lancaster -Manchester which left here an hour ago. I know this because I checked my timepiece just before getting into it."

John Nicholson laughed, "No Jonty. That is impossible. Now let's dress that head wound of yours." Jonty sat by the fireside and pondered on the last hour. After making enquires with the other hotel guests, no one could confirm the arrival of the second coach.

Well, we do know that the following day Jonty did get home to Bromley Cross and that evening watched his daughter enter the world.

What Jonty never did know was that two years previously, the Manchester coach had left the Swan Hotel and came off the road in appalling weather conditions. The coach fell in to the ravine at Jeffrey Hill, Longridge, killing the six horses, driver, two women and a baby.

Did Jonty Martindale climb on to a ghost coach that night? It has been said that on moonlit winter nights the sound of a coach can be heard making its way along the old West Riding lanes. Could this be the Lancaster - Manchester coach that never completed its ill fated journey in 1880?

Chapter 2
The Taxi

Ibrahim Khan browsed through the pages of the Exchange and Mart magazine as he did each month. He was looking for a bargain. Suddenly his eyes lit up, as he noticed a Ford Granada estate for sale. The vehicle had only run up some 5,000 miles and the seller, a Bolton garage wanted £4,000 for it.

"A bargain!" he whispered. He shouted to his father and brother, "Look at this car! It's just what we need - full service history, and really low mileage. Father, I must go and look at the car tomorrow."

"I agree," his father said. Ibrahim set of from his home on Whalley Range on the outskirts of Blackburn, driving over the moors through Darwen, then into Bolton. He drove through the town centre and glanced at the sat nav.

"Next corner," he muttered, "Ah there's the garage." He pulled onto the garage forecourt and parked up. He made his way to the shop situated on the forecourt, inside there was a short, stocky man called John Hodson. He was wearing a blue boiler suit and had a balding head.

"Excuse me please," said Ibrahim, "I understand you have a Granada estate for sale?"

"Aye, I do lad." said the stocky man, "I have only purchased it and given it a thorough service. It's not a bad car, and it's got really low mileage."

"Please could I test drive it Sir?" Said Ibrahim.

"Aye okay lad. I'll get keys," he said in a strong Bolton accent. The two of them climbed into the estate car. Ibrahim turned the key and the vehicle's engine fired first time. He indicated, left the forecourt, and they drove a few miles into the town centre. "You have a bargain here, lad."

"I agree!" said Ibrahim. "But can I ask you please, why do you want to sell this car for £4.000? It must be worth more, after all, it is only twenty-four months old."

"The truth is, I need a quick sale lad. In my business you have to sell quick, you understand." He explained as he placed some tobacco snuff on his hand and snorted up the tobacco. They drove back to the garage.

"I'll get the paperwork for you," he said as Ibrahim watched the stocky man go in to the office sneezing wildly after his intake of snuff. He came back to Ibrahim.

"Right lad, let's talk money." Ibrahim reached into his daughter's school satchel that he had borrowed for this occasion. He opened it and pulled out a huge wad of cash. The garage owner's eyes lit up with glee.

"I will have to count it lad." A few moments later he smiled.

"Okay lad that's four grand, the car's yours."

Ibrahim telephoned his brother Masar, to confirm the sale, and he arranged to pick up Ibrahim's car whilst Ibrahim drove the Granada back to Blackburn. Once home, he, his brother and father Ali looked at the car.

"You have a bargain Ibrahim. Well done! We now need to get the vehicle Hackney licensed."

The following day the local council granted them a license after seeing all the correct paperwork. A radio was fitted and the family now had three registered taxis. Ibrahim and his family worked all hours to make a living. They had run the business for the previous ten years.

The competition in Blackburn was intense, and in order to make a living they had no choice but to put the time in. By far the most lucrative work came on a Friday night and the Whalley run. Whalley had the only night club in the Ribble Valley, and hordes of young people would travel from Blackburn, Burnley and Clitheroe to the night club. Ibrahim pulled up in Clitheroe town centre, and almost immediately three mini-skirted young ladies climbed into the back of the Granada. Ibrahim was a strict Muslim, and detected the strong aroma of alcohol, but in his trade he understood that on nights like these, he would expect many similar passengers. On some occasions he would get some aggressive persons due to alcohol abuse, and had been subjected to not only racist remarks but also physical abuse.

His father had recently had a nasty confrontation in Burnley when three youths refused to pay their fare and ran into a darkened street. He ran after them and they set about him, knocking a tooth out and leaving him in a painful and somewhat sad state.

Ibrahim arrived in the village of Whalley and his passengers paid their fare and ran giggling in to the night club. He picked up the radio mike in the cab and contacted his sister in Blackburn.

"Any trade Shanaz?" he enquired,

"I have Ibrahim. Billington to Darwen," said his sister, who operated the phones.

"Thanks," he said and shortly after, he arrived in Billington at the address given and picked a couple up. He was quite relieved they were not drunk, but were in fact quite pleasant to talk to. He arrived in Darwen at the Entwistle Arms, and again contacted Shanazz.

"Hi. Any more trade, Sister?"

"This has just come in Ibrahim, could you go to Turton and take three people to Blackburn town centre."

He set off towards Turton and the journey over the moors. His passengers paid their fares and he then looked at the time on the dashboard clock. It read 1.30 am.

"That must be the last job for the night," he said as he set off for home. As he drove through Blackburn town centre, he glanced up at his rear view mirror. A car was advancing at great speed, overtaking him in a thirty mph zone. As the car sped past, two youths made two fingered gestures at him as their car overtook the taxi. He recognised the car as being from his own neighbourhood, "I bet they're on drugs," he muttered. He then glanced up at the rear view mirror again, and noticed to his shock and horror, that he was staring into the eyes of a grey-haired elderly woman wearing round spectacles. She was sitting in the middle of the back seat. Ibrahim shrieked in terror. He knew she was not there a few minutes ago and he had certainly not stopped to pick her up.

The taxi screeched to a halt, Ibrahim jumped out of the vehicle and ran a few yards away. He reached into his jeans for a pack of cigarettes, placed one between his lips and nervously reached into his other pocket for the lighter. He then turned around and plucked up the courage to look into the back of the vehicle. To his relief there was nobody there. He stroked his forehead and inhaled deeply. He could not believe what he had just witnessed. He reached into the cab's front window and picked up the radio mike.

"Shanaz, please come in."

"Okay Ibrahim. Are you okay?" she enquired.

"No!" he said. Shanaz shouted back,

"Have you been attacked?"

"No," he replied. "I have just seen a ghost." His sister laughed.

"Have you been inhaling alcohol fumes?" she said sarcastically.

"No, this woman was sitting in the back, I looked in the rear mirror. She stared straight into my eyes!"

Shanaz could tell by the tone of his voice that he was indeed very serious.

"I cannot drive this car home!" he shouted down the mike.

"Okay, calm down Ibrahim. I will ask Masar to collect the car and you can drive back in his."

"Thank you sister," he replied gratefully. Ibrahim's brother Masar arrived twenty minutes later in a foul mood.

"What the bloody hell is wrong? I was in bed!"

"Masar, I swear to you this car is haunted," pleaded Ibrahim.

Masar replied, "Bollocks. You have been seeing things. I will drive it home, you take my car." The two of them left Blackburn town centre for the area known as Whalley Range where they lived.

The following morning, Ibrahim told his father what had happened the previous night.

"You need some sleep son. You have been overdoing it. I will take the Granada out tonight, you take my car. We have just spent four thousand pounds on that vehicle. We must make it pay, we have a business to run." That night was a typical Saturday evening in East Lancashire, and all three taxis were on the road. Ibrahim's father Ali picked up the mike.

"Shanaz any trade my dear?"

"Yes father. Could you go to Waddington village and pick up four people heading for Billington?"

Ali drove to the picturesque village of Waddington and was delighted when his passengers seemed to be very sober. He drove the four miles to Billington, collected the fare, and started the journey back to Blackburn. He turned the car radio on to the local Asian station, and suddenly felt he was not alone. He instantly looked up into the rear view mirror. There his eyes looked into a grey-haired woman's face. She was wearing glasses. She almost smiled at him.

Ali Screamed out loud, and the taxi mounted the pavement. In a state of pure terror and panic, Ali opened the driver side door at great speed to escape the car. His thoughts were with his son Ibrahim. He realised that he had indeed been speaking the truth. He reached for his mobile phone.

"Masar, please could you pick up the car I am just north of Wilpshire."

Masar shouted, "What's wrong father?"

"I have seen Ibrahim's ghost. She scared the shit out of me, I am not driving this car again."

Masar arrived again. "Okay Dad, you drive my car - I will drive the Granada. This is getting to be a habit."

The following day Shanaz had the job of vacuuming each vehicle and cleaning the windows and seating. All three cars were on the pavement outside the family home. She happily started her chores and began to clean the front windows and dashboard of the Granada. She sprayed the dash, then she started to clean the rear view mirror. Suddenly her blood froze as she gazed into the eyes of an old woman in spectacles and grey hair. Screaming in utter panic, she ran into the house and straight into her father's arms.

"What's wrong my girl?" asked an alarmed Ali. Shanaz blurted out and described what she had seen.

"Right!" shouted Ali, "that car is going back to Bolton - we will sell it back." Ibrahim and Masar both agreed.

"Yes father, the car is cursed. We will never drive it again. The following morning Masar bravely got behind the controls of the Granada. His father and brother took one of the other taxis, and they set off for Bolton and John Hodson's garage.

To Masar's delight, the journey was uneventful and he sighed with relief as he parked the estate car on the garage forecourt. Hodson watched the trio advance towards his office, with a grin on his face. From the look on their faces, he knew they were on a mission. As they entered his premises, he shouted,

"There is nowt wrong with that car, it has a full service record, low mileage and it's got a brand new wing. You've got an absolute bargain."

"We have decided that this is not the car we need. Please will you buy it back?" asked Ibrahim as politely as possible.

Ali enquired, "A new wing you say. Why?"

Well, Hodson looked a bit sheepish and nervously informed them that the car had been involved in a serious road traffic accident where an elderly lady had been killed on the back seat. The three of them were stunned by this information.

"Yes," Hodson said wearily, "I have last year's Bolton Evening News in my office regarding the accident." He opened his filing cabinet and fished around for the old newspaper, found it and opened the second page. And there was a photograph of an elderly woman. Ali and Ibrahim looked at each other in shock as they both recognised the face in the paper as the same face that had stared at them through the rear view mirror in the Granada.

"I'll tell you what lads. I will give you two grand for it."

"Okay! Done!" said Ali. Hodson laughed to himself.

This was the eighth time in three months that he had sold the car and its ghostly occupant. He knew the car would always be returned, and a healthy profit was to be made.

Chapter 3
The Ghost Soldier

The Clitheroe Territorials waited outside the parish church office building for a platoon photograph. The tallest were at the back and the shortest at the front. The photographer raised his voice.

"Okay lads, stand very still." There was a dazzling flash. "That's fine boys, thank you," he shouted. It was September 1939 and the Territorials had all been called up as part of the British Expeditionary Force. The Unit consisted of fifty-seven young men. There was raw excitement in the air.

"This is gripping stuff!" muttered 19 year old Lance Corporal Billy Lakin. He and his mates were only too happy to get out of the textile mills and the chance to go abroad, and add some excitement to their lives. The company made their way to the railway station. Mothers, wives and girlfriends had a last hug on the platform. Bill felt a slight lump in his throat as his parents gave him a concerned look.

"Bill, look after yourself!" his mother said.

"You will write won't you son?" His father nervously asked.

In a whoosh of steam and smoke the train pulled out of Clitheroe station, taking its khaki, steel-helmeted passengers to the south coast. There, they made the journey across the English Channel.

Bill was nudged by his mate Pat Crompton.

"Do you think we will ever see Clitheroe again Bill?"

"Yeah, course we will! We will be in the White Lion by Christmas!" he said confidently.

The Clitheroe detachment joined their battalion, the East Lancashire Regiment, and were dispatched to the Maginot Line, French fortifications. On arriving, they were told by the Colonel,

"Don't worry boys. These defences are the most secure in the world the Germans will never be able to get through them. It's impossible!"

Well, the unit spent the next eight months in the line, and not a shot was fired. Each side seemed to be happy to just sit and wait. But this all changed on the 10th of May 1940, when the German military launched Blitzkrieg lightening war. Bill and the Clitheroe detachment were shocked to find the German armed forces did not bother attacking the Maginot Line. They just went around the back of it. The Company Commander Lieutenant Parker shouted,

"Right, lads! Get your weapons and as much ammunition as you can carry. We are leaving."

"Why, Sir?" Bill asked.

"There's a real flap on. We have to get out of here as soon as possible. The Germans are hot on our tail. Leave your great coats and other equipment we need to move fast. The company double-marched through the French countryside.

Pat shouted above the noise of hobnailed boots and the clinking of mess tins,

"I need a rest Bill, I cannot keep this up."

"Keep going!" shouted the Lieutenant, "We need to get as much distance as possible behind us from the German's advance."

Due to the speed of the march the boys broke into a heavy sweat and water bottles began to dry up.

They marched all day and into the night, through the French countryside. Lieutenant Parker said,

"Right lads, get off the road, and we will have a couple of hours rest by the hedgerow. Lance Corporal Lakin, get your Bren gun positioned behind us. You can have the first watch. As his comrades fell into a deep sleep on the roadside verge, Bill extended the Bren gun's tripod, put a fresh magazine into the breech, and took up the firing position behind the weapon.

He could feel the weight of tiredness on him. But he was on guard and if he fell asleep he would be court-marshalled. He gazed down the Bren's sight, because in the far distance he could see a dot on the road. The dot got closer and materialised into a motorbike dispatch rider. Its engine woke the lieutenant, and a huge smile came across the riders face.

"Thank God you're British!" Lieutenant Parker shouted.

"Do you know where the East Lancashire battalion is Sir? The whole B.E.F has orders to go straight to Dunkirk for evacuation," said the motorcycle rider.

"What? That's absurd!" said Parker, "What's happened?" The lieutenant asked the dispatch rider.

"Sir. I understand the Germans have broken through Belgium and France and will be here where we are standing in a matter of hours."

"Right, get up all of you, men. I don't care how tired you are we are going straight to Dunkirk," shouted the lieutenant. Exhausted and very hungry and footsore the platoon arrived at the channel port of Dunkirk. The town was on fire by the time the Clitheroe Company arrived. Bill felt like death warmed up. He had not eaten in four days and had also not slept. The company made their way onto the sand dunes. All they could see in every direction were thousands of B.E.F. soldiers, all with the same dazed and confused look on their faces. Bill took off his tin helmet and as his body made contact with the sand, he fell in to a deep, exhausted sleep. This was his first sleep in 82 hours. But this much-needed sleep was interrupted a short time later by a horrific noise. The Luftwaffe had decided to pay a visit, and the dreaded Stuka dive bombers came screaming down from the blue sky above them. A Stuka came right down the beach with its machine guns pumping bullets in Bill's direction. He spread himself on the sand dune, pointing his helmet in the direction of the attacking plane.

The Stuka flew over him, its siren creating a sound

of pure horror. Bill suddenly became aware of screaming, and as he got to his feet, he could make out his pal Pat Crompton on his knees gripping his abdomen. Pat's battledress jacket was soaked in blood. Bill ran to him and shouted, "Pat, we will get you sorted mate." Pat turned to him, his face twisted and grey with agony,

"I don't think so mate."

As Bill supported his best pal, he became aware that Pat had a huge hole in his back, the result of one of the Stuka's bullets. Pat Crompton's limp body slipped from Bill's support. These two had been at primary school together. Pat was not going to see his twentieth birthday or indeed any other birthday.

"What can I tell his mother?" Bill whispered to himself. Suddenly Lieutenant Parker's voice shouted.

"Clitheroe platoon, to me now! Right lads use your helmets, we need to dig in to the sand dunes to escape these air raids."

"Any food or water Sir?" asked one lad.

"No I am afraid not. We will have to make do. I understand the navy want to take us all off the beach and back home across the channel. We just have to wait."

The Luftwaffe came four more times that day, bringing death to the unprotected boys on the beach.

"Where the bloody hell is the Royal Air Force?" shouted a Welsh guardsman. Lieutenant Parker had been invited to a staff meeting, and came back with a smile on his face.

He shouted into the dunes, "Clitheroe platoon, to me now!" The company gathered round. "Right lads," said the lieutenant, "It's our turn to be evacuated. Let's get down to the beach, keep your rifles above your heads!"

The Clitheroe Platoon eagerly made their way to the water's edge and waded in. Bill held the Bren gun above the salt water, and the company found themselves neck deep in the English Channel. Suddenly a Stuka flew in at low level, the pilot pressed his gun sight and a hail of lead found their targets. The Clitheroe Company tried to get out of the water, but many were caught by the Stuka's firepower.

Bill instantly dived beneath the cold waves, as he came to the surface the water around him was crimson with the blood of his company. He suddenly heard a voice. He turned round and a small boat was a few inches away from him. A Royal Navy officer grabbed his battledress collar and dragged him on board the vessel. He had lost the Bren gun, but the fact he was alive and in one piece, was a joy.

The small vessel took him to a destroyer bound for Dover. On board Bill received the best meal he had ever consumed, a corned beef sandwich, a mug of hot tea and a players cigarette.

On arriving in Dover he was informed by an officer, "Right, we all know where you have come from. Just go home you do not need a ticket for your rail journey. Go home, register with your T.A. battalion and await orders."

Bill walked along the Dover jetty and could not see any of his Clitheroe Company.

"Did they get away?" he muttered.

Soon he was on the northern train. He had time to look at himself in the train's WC mirror. His battledress was in tatters, he was unshaven and he also noticed that his big toe was actually pointing out of his toe cap. Due to the forced march from the Maginot line to Dunkirk, the leather on his boots soles were paper thin. The train at last pulled in to his home town of Clitheroe on a beautiful May night. Bill got out of the carriage and kissed the railway platform.

"I am home," he whispered. His instinct was to go straight to his parent's home on Pimlico Road, but he remembered his orders from Lieutenant Parker.

"Get back to the Parish church office at all costs."

Bill was elated to be alive, but this elation was short lived as he thought of Pat's horrible death on the beaches.

And how he had to go and tell his parents that they had lost their son. Bill hobbled up to the Parish church office on Church Street. He opened the door, and inside he discovered that out of the fifty-seven young men who had left last September, only nineteen, himself included, had made it back home. They registered their names and Battalion were informed.

A few days later, a meeting took place at the parish office drill hall. "The Clitheroe Company must be made up to company strength," said the Battalion's Colonel. In those days, if you were eighteen years old, you were conscripted - but if you were seventeen, you could join up with your parent's consent.

Bill was made up to full corporal. He was just nineteen years old by this time. He had a pal who was only seventeen called John Grimes. John kept pestering his parents, "Please sign this consent form, I want to fight for my country!" But his parents insisted that he was indeed too young. John's persistence seemed to pay off when his parents reluctantly gave in to his requests.

However there was one catch. John's mother and father insisted that Bill should look after him like a brother. Bill swore that he would take him under his wing and protect him in times of danger.

John Grimes signed up, went through his military training and became a member of the newly formed Clitheroe platoon. In 1941 they were posted to the beautiful Greek island of Crete. There they made up the British garrison along with units of Australian and New Zealand forces.

On the 21st of May 1941 the Germans invaded Crete with an aerial invasion using paratroops and glider-born infantry. The German troops where all very well equipped and highly professional, the British and Commonwealth troops were very poorly equipped, but put up stiff resistance with what they had.

The Maori Troops in particular fought extremely well inflicting huge losses on the Germans. The Mallarme Aerodrome became the main objective of the conflict from the German perspective, and the New Zealand General Freyberg could not hold it, due to the limited amount of men at his disposal.

Bill gazed down the Bren gun's sight, the heat from the mid-day sun was extreme. The Clitheroe platoon were all dripping with sweat as they dug slit trenches in the olive groves not too far away from the aerodrome. Suddenly German mortar fire came raining in. "Get your heads down lads!" shouted Captain Lockett, the Company Commander. "We can expect an infantry attack at any minute!"

White hot shrapnel filled the air. The platoon hugged the earth in the trenches. Seventeen year old John Grimes felt very nervous indeed. He had never come across the horrors of war before. Bill put his hand on his back, "Don't worry pal," he said reassuringly. "The Bren will scare the Jerries away." In the distance the platoon heard screams and shouting and a strange noise. Suddenly a group of Australian troops came running past their positions.

"They have got a bloody flame thrower!" They shouted, "It's done for half of our mates." The Aussies continued shouting and yelling, "Run lads save yourselves!"

Captain Locket, the Company Commander shouted, "No men, we stay here!" The horrific sound of the flame thrower got closer, squirting burning liquid in their direction.

Bill shouted to young Grimes, "John, run back to the ammunition truck. Hide behind the tail board, its metal will shield you. The seventeen year old's face was contorted with horror as he jumped out of the slit trench and ran over open ground in the direction of the ammunition truck. The German troops started closing in on the Clitheroe Company's position and sniper fire was heard as Grimes ran as fast as his legs would carry him over open ground.

Bill watched in horror as he witnessed Grimes suddenly stop in his tracks. For a second he stood motionless, and then fell down in the fettle position, "Oh Christ - he has been hit!" shouted one of the lads.

Bill got to his feet and ran to where Grimes lay, on reaching him he was distraught to see that the young lad had a neat bullet hole in his forehead. He had died instantly. Bill was gripped in total shock and emotional trauma. He had let the lad's parents down, and himself.

"How can I live with this?" he muttered. A bullet whizzed past his nose.

Sergeant Proctor shouted, "Get back here Lakin! Leave him!" Bill ran back to the slit trench in a state of shock. He could not believe what he had just taken in.

"Right lads. Open fire!" shouted Captain Lockett. The Paratroopers came into view, armed to the teeth - one squirting flame in their direction.

"Lakin! Take him out!" shouted Captain Lockett. Bill swung the Bren gun round and pulled the
butt into his shoulder. He aimed and squeezed the trigger and the Bren kicked, firing rounds towards the flame thrower and its operative.

Suddenly there erupted a huge orange flash as the Bren guns bullets hit the operative's tanks on his back containing the highly flammable liquid. The paratrooper screamed as he literally burnt to death, his comrades taking cover amongst the olive trees.

Bill shouted to the lads around him, "Have any of you got any Bren magazines? I only have one left." Captain Locket was furious.

"How the hell do they expect us to hold with ammunition restrictions?"

The vast majority of troops on Crete had been evacuated from Greece and had only a few rounds each.
Sergeant Proctor shouted, "Lads, use every round and make sure you kill each time!" For the next hour they exchanged fire with the paratroopers. Eventually Bill emptied his last magazine at the German positions.

"Right men," shouted Captain Lockett. "We have our rifles. Fix bayonets!" he screamed. The enemy became aware that the tommies had no ammunition left, and encircled the Clitheroe positions.

One man on Bill's right muttered, "We don't stand a bloody chance!"

Suddenly they heard from the undergrowth a voice, "You have fought bravely, we offer you the option of surrendering," in perfect English.

Lockett looked around him. "We have no ammunition left, some of my men have wives and children, our position is fruitless."

The Captain stood up in view of the enemy with raised hands. "We surrender." He announced. The enemy were on them in seconds. A German Corporal patted the soldier's pockets as they stood in a long line.

The Lieutenant commanding the German section looked down at the body of seventeen year old John Grimes. He turned to Captain Lockett. "Why do you send children in to battle? This is a boy. Are things so desperate in England that you send children to their deaths?" The captain made no comment but silently agreed. The Clitheroe Platoon were sent to the airfield to be transported to a P.O.W camp.

Three months later, the Platoon found themselves in Poland. Bill felt extreme guilt for the death of young Grimes and blamed himself entirely. By sending him to the ammunition truck, the boy's fate was sealed. Had he stayed with Bill, he would probably still be alive. From his P.O.W camp, through the Red Cross he wrote a series of letters to Mr and Mrs Grimes in Clitheroe, begging their forgiveness for their son's death. Letters came back via the Red Cross, from the lad's parents.

"Bill, we do not blame you for our son's death. We do forgive you, do not blame yourself. Those years as a P.O.W were long and very depressing. Bill's weight went down to 8 stone, and young Grimes' death haunted him every night.

In 1945 Bill finally got home to Clitheroe. He did not celebrate with his fellow P.O.W's, and he felt that he could never look Mr and Mrs Grimes in the face ever again. However Bill did marry and worked at the local cement factory. But everyday his memory went back to Crete and that tragic day in 1941. For years Bill carried this burden of guilt.

Bill had no idea that his life was going to change on the 24th of December 1968. It was Christmas Eve and he made his way up to the parish church office, the old T.A. hall to watch the Clitheroe amateur operatic societies Christmas play. He was the last person to leave the building. As he stood outside and lit a cigarette, he looked at the front of the building. The very scene of that photograph taken of the Clitheroe territorials in 1939. He sighed, extinguished the cigarette with his foot and took a left turn to walk down "Paradise Lane," the alleyway down the side of the building, down to York Street.

Suddenly, he heard a whisper "Bill. Bill. Billy." He turned round and some two feet behind him he saw young Grimes in his British Army uniform. The boy had a huge smile on his face, "Bill, don't worry about me mate. I am fine. Don't worry." He repeated. The hair on the back of Bill's neck stood up as he realised he was looking into the face of a ghost. His legs gave way and he knelt on the cobble stones in the alleyway. In his own words, he bellowed like a wounded animal. The boy raised his ghostly arm, and again repeated, with a sympathetic look, "Bill, I am fine. Don't worry about me." The ghostly character then turned, smiled, waved and vaporised into the night air.

Bill slowly got to his feet with tears streaming down his face. He walked home past all the happy Christmas revellers. The last thing on Bill's mind was Christmas - he was deeply upset and traumatised by what he had just experienced. He got home and climbed into bed and fell into a very deep sleep. The sort of sleep he had not experienced in years.

Some hours later, he was woken by the Christmas morning bells of Saint James', Saint Mary's and Saint

Peter's churches. He got out of bed and felt at complete ease with himself. He had not felt as good in years, if ever. He entered the bathroom and caught his reflection in the mirror. He looked again and again, and noticed a change in his facial expression. He was actually smiling. Something he had not done for over twenty five years, since 1941 in fact.

Bill felt that he had at last been forgiven for the death of seventeen year old John Grimes.

Chapter 4
The Sough Tunnel

Miles Whitelock loved the railway that linked his home town of Darwen with the city of Manchester. His house and back garden faced the railway line, and Miles would spend many days waving at the steam locomotive drivers as they made their journeys up and down the line. He told his parents, "One day I am going to drive a steam locomotive, I want a job on the railway." He left school at fourteen and was delighted to get a job with the East Lancashire Railway, as a wheel tapper, and at the age of eighteen he became a fireman - shovelling coal into the furnace of the locomotives.

Just after his twenty-second birthday, Miles was delighted to train and qualify as a driver. His dream had come true and he would travel all over the London Midland Scottish region on a class of engine known as a Black 5. In the summer of 1962 he was delighted to be transferred to his native East Lancashire area, and as he went past his parent's home he would pull the whistle cable three times to let his parents know that he was driving through.

One beautiful August morning Miles took some rolling stock up to Carlisle, then brought some freight down to Manchester. This route would take him through the Sough Tunnel. Opened in 1854, the lads who built it had to literally hammer through solid rock for some two miles with pickaxes and shovels. As Miles was about to enter the tunnel from the Darwen end he noticed in the field behind the wire fence, a young boy with almost straw coloured hair, waving and smiling at him. Miles reached for the whistle cable and made three impressive hoots, to the delight of the boy who jumped up and down with excitement.

That summer Miles made many journeys down the line, the straw-colour haired boy was always waiting for him, and would make the same gesture by pulling at an invisible whistle cord. Miles got used to this, every day at the same time.

Towards the end of August, Miles took his Black 5 down to Manchester. He looked for the little boy, and noticed he was in a different part of the field. On seeing the familiar locomotive the boy started to run towards the fence. Miles looked on in amazement as the boy was actually running through sleeping sheep as if they were not solid. The sheep didn't seem to know he was there. The hair on Miles' neck rose. He realized that he had just witnessed something very paranormal.

The Black 5 entered the Sough Tunnel. Miles shouted to his fireman, "Did you see that?"

"No mate," he replied. "I was shoveling."

Miles was somewhat stunned, "I cannot believe what I have just witnessed!"

The Black 5 entered the city of Manchester's Victoria station, to deliver their freight and prepare to take new freight up north. Once the freight was coupled they popped into the station buffet bar, for tea and a sandwich. The fireman enquired, "Miles you have been quiet mate, what's wrong?"

"It's that little lad near the tunnel entrance, he ran along the side of the railway fence, and through the sleeping sheep!"

The fireman laughed, "You're seeing things mate."

They finished their break and got back to the marshalling yard. The fireman started to get a good fire going under the boiler. Once they had full steam they started off on the journey up the line to Blackburn. Miles felt somewhat apprehensive as the train made its way up to the Sough Tunnel. In the far distance near the entrance he could see a figure standing in the centre of the line. He slowed the Black 5 down, and the figure came into view. It was a police officer holding a red lamp in his hand. The other hand was in the air signaling the driver to stop. With a whoosh of steam the Black 5 came to a halt.

"What's wrong officer?" shouted Miles.

The officer had a distressed look on his face, "Oh, it's very sad," muttered the policeman. "The same family!"

"Same family?" Miles asked with an enquiring look.

"Yes, some nine years ago a little lad was killed at the other end of the tunnel. His brother was killed this afternoon in the same place. I feel for the parents." said the officer with a desperately sad expression on his face.

Suddenly word came down the line,

"You have permission to continue your journey."

"Thank you officer," said Miles and the engine made its way through the two miles of tunnel. Eventually, the end was in sight, which was always a relief as the smoke could make breathing unpleasant. The Black 5 emerged into the sunlight. Miles instinctively glanced to his left as he always did to acknowledge the little boy. The boy with the bright straw-coloured hair was there. But this time, he was holding the hand of a much taller lad. Both youths waved at Miles, as the train passed them and then they vaporised into thin air.

Miles' heart thumped in his chest as he exhaled, deeply. "Oh my God!" he whispered. He shouted to his fireman, "Did you see that?"

The response again was, "Sorry mate, too busy shovelling."

Miles spent another 24 years on the railway, He never saw the ghosts again, but he never forgot his ghostly encounter in 1962. To this day the Sough Tunnel has a very spooky atmosphere and is a monument to the many men who lost their lives during its construction.

Chapter 5
The Move

Joe Briggs had just celebrated his eighth birthday. His mum and dad had done everything to make his birthday special, a cake and a party. But Joe did have a twinge of sadness in him. This was not only his birthday, but also a leaving party.

His father Ian had been promoted in his job as a personnel officer and had been transferred to an office in Kendal, Westmorland.

His father said, "Joe, I have bought this beautiful old house just outside the Lake District. It has a huge garden, and not too far from Lake Windermere and the coast."

Joe put on a brave smile, he had no option. He said goodbye to his many friends, and as he hugged them, he secretly knew that it was very likely that he would never see them again.

Nottingham was a huge city. Joe had been to many a Notts' County football match with his father and also to Trent Bridge for the cricket. Nottingham was his home and yes it did hurt to have to leave the city and his many friends. The Pickford's removal vehicle arrived and his mum and dad excitedly helped the removal staff put the many tea chests in to the vehicle. It was soon full of the family's entire possessions.

"We will follow in the car," said Joe's father. To the Foreman, Nottingham to Westmorland was a long journey, some four hours at least. Joe went back into his empty home for the last time and with a huge lump in his throat and a tear welling up in his eye, he looked at his bedroom wall for the very last time, and the familiar wallpaper with its Superman figures. How excited he had been when his mum bought the paper and as he watched his parents decorate the room. He also looked at a patch near the door and a crayon mark that he had made at the age of four.

Suddenly a voice shouted from downstairs, "Come on Joe, we have to go now love." shouted his mum. Joe could not hold back the emotion any more and burst into tears. He felt a sympathetic hug from his mum, "Come on dear," she said affectionately. "You will love the countryside."

They started the long journey up north, keeping just behind the Pickford's vehicle. His dad was concerned about Joe, and not only bought him some fruit gums, but promised him fishing trips on the lake.

"And we can both join the Carlisle United supporters club." He offered, trying to take the boy's mind off the upheaval.

The family's new home in Westmorland was situated in a hamlet called Greenside. This consisted of a beautiful old mansion built in 1898 and converted into three new dwellings. The removal vehicle pulled up in front of the mansion. Joe's dad had bought the west wing; it had a huge lawn the size of three football pitches, and the driveway up to the house had an avenue of rhododendron and holly bushes on both sides.

The countryside surrounding the hamlet was simply stunning. A short walk would take you on to a place called Heversham Head, and the views from the top on the Head were panoramic and outstanding. The River Kent meandered into Morecambe Bay and the Irish Sea. All around, the Lake District peaks and mountains came into view. Joe's dad inhaled deeply with a huge smile on his face.

"Taste that air," he said. "It's good enough to eat!" He was elated, along with his new job and home, he had also had a huge increase in salary. That had enabled him to buy the house. His wife Jean was also delighted with their new home. They made their way inside. The house had a huge kitchen, it was four times bigger than their Nottingham home. It had a reception room and a dining room, and upstairs there were four bedrooms with plenty of room.

The removal staff emptied the vehicle, taking items

of furniture to their designated areas.

"Sign here please, Mr Briggs," said the Foreman. The Pickford's vehicle made its way down the drive and began the long journey back to the city of Nottingham.

Young Joe ran upstairs to the third floor to explore, and entered what he hoped would be his new bedroom. This room was huge and faced the front of the house. He looked out of the window. The views took in the huge lawn in the front of the property and magnificent rolling countryside, with a multitude of lanes all with rows of hedges. As he gazed from the window out into the countryside, Joe suddenly had the feeling that he was being watched. He nervously turned round and the door behind him slowly closed as if something had just brushed past. He ran towards the door to run downstairs to the kitchen where his parents were emptying the tea chests. He grabbed the door knob, and for a second felt he heard a scratching noise and what sounded like a dog's bark. He flung the door open, to find that there was no-one there. But he did sense the aroma of wet dog. He ran down all three flights of stairs, and dashed into the kitchen, almost knocking his mum over.

"What's wrong Joe?" she said in an alarmed voice.

"I think there's a dog in the house," pleaded the young lad.

"No," said his dad, "there are just the three of us," his father calmly explained. "Well Joe, its time to get you to bed - this has been a very long day."

Joe's bed was quickly assembled and the mattress placed on it. His mum very quickly made up the bed, and Joe got in, and fell asleep almost as soon as he had placed his head on the pillow. The long journey had worn him out and Joe had very quickly fallen into a deep sleep.

Downstairs his mum and dad started to empty all the cutlery and other utensils, and by midnight, they too were exhausted by the journey and the stress associated with a house move.

"Let's make up our bed dear," said Jean. Ian grabbed the spanner and tightened the bolts on the bed legs and the head board. The weary pair climbed into bed.

Outside, bright moonlight was illuminating the house. They were too tired to put up the curtains. That was a job that could wait as this was a country house and there were no neighbouring houses where people could look into the room. Both of them were asleep in minutes.

A few hours later, Ian suddenly woke up as he heard a noise. He heard the sound of tiny footsteps coming up the stairs towards his bedroom. Ian felt a sense of panic as the bedroom door slowly opened and to his astonishment, in came a white cocker spaniel. The dog made its way to the corner of the bedroom and sat in the bright moonlight that was shining through the bedroom window. Ian wondered how the dog got into the house.

"I must have left a door open downstairs," he muttered as he flung the sheets back and got out of bed. He walked towards the spaniel. "Come on, let's have you!" he said and attempted to grab the creature's collar. To Ian's horror, his hand went straight through the dog. He made a second attempt, and once again his hand was clutching at thin air. He gasped in shock, and sat on the bed, his heart racing.

Still staring at the spaniel, the dog seemed to glance to the left, as if it heard a command. To Ian's amazement the animal just vaporised into thin air. At that exact moment his wife Jean woke up with a jolt from a deep sleep.

"Oh Ian! I have just had a most unusual dream, a very clear dream," she said. "There was a man outside the house looking up at our bedroom window. He was wearing clothing from the Victorian period, top hat and tails. In his hand, he had a dog lead and seemed to be making hand gestures at something in the bedroom."

For a second Ian's blood froze in his body. He told his wife Jean what had happened in the past minute. The both of them looked each other in the eye as they realised that they had just experienced a paranormal event. In the years that followed every new owner of number 1, Greenside, Heversham, would receive a visit from this ghostly spaniel on their first night at the residence.

Why does he appear? Could he just be welcoming the new owners to this fine Victorian building? The house was built in 1898 and the original owners had their own hounds and gun dogs. Perhaps the spaniel loved the house so much, he could not leave.

Chapter 6
The Western Gate House, Whalley Abbey

John Hesketh was born at the wrong time of the last century. He started attending Whalley Primary School in 1904. His best friend was called Annie Creswell, and she helped him with his homework, and sometimes filled in his text books in class.

By the time these two were sixteen years old, they were indeed an item. At the age of eighteen, they married at All Saints Church in Whalley, and had a marvellous honeymoon on the beautiful Isle of Man.

On returning home to Whalley, John was horrified to find a crisp letter on his doormat with the words "Ministry of Defence" stamped on the envelope.

"Bloody hell! It's my call-up papers," he said. "I have no gripe with the Germans!" he shouted, "I haven't a clue what this war is about. I don't want to join up, I have just got married!" he cried out. But he knew he had no option. He had been conscripted and that was that. He hugged young Annie, and gave her a huge kiss. "I will be back love, don't worry."

He made his way to Rose Grove barracks in Burnley and for the next twelve weeks, he bulled his boots, pressed his khaki uniform, and learnt how to fire and clean his 303 Lee Enfield rifle.

He was delighted to learn that he had the luxury of two days leave with his beloved wife Annie. John felt such euphoria just to kiss and hold her, and that night he made love to her, sadly for the last time. John and Annie had no idea but Annie conceived that night. He knew deep inside his heart that he would never see Annie again or indeed the beautiful village of Whalley. But, he did not want to upset his wife. He put on a brave face, but the pain he felt, as he climbed aboard the train at Whalley railway station was exceptionally hard for a young man of eighteen years old to take in.

The train pulled out of the station. John looked back from the railway carriage into the eyes of his young wife, and whispered through the steam and smoke, "Goodbye my love."

His battalion, the East Lancashires, marched up the line, the date being July the 1st 1916, the first day of the Somme Offensive. John had no idea that some eighty thousand other British and Commonwealth boys were doing just the same. The British Generals had organised a huge assault on the German positions and had told all of their officers, "It will be a piece of cake boys!"

The Sergeant Major shouted, "Right lads. I want you all to write a letter to your loved ones." John wrote a quick letter to young Annie back in Whalley. He licked the envelope and after writing the address gave it to the Sergeant Major as indeed all the other lads did. The Platoon's letters were then skewered by a bayonet and placed in a sand bag at the top of the trench.

"You will be in Berlin by Christmas!" shouted the warrant officer.

At Exactly 7.30 am on the 1st of July 1916, the assault was launched. John Heskett lit a cigarette, and placed the packet back in his breast pocket. Behind the cigarette packet was a photograph of Annie in her wedding dress. Quite a few of his platoon had admired her, each telling him that he was so lucky to have such a bonnie lass for a wife. The British artillery had been shelling the enemy trenches for three days and nights. They were told that the enemy positions will have huge casualties and the barbed wire will also be destroyed. The enemy trenches that John and his mates were going to attack had been constructed very deep and also had railway sleepers on top to absorb heavy shelling.

That day was going to be the blackest day in the history of the British Armed Forces. Suddenly the shelling stopped and the East Lancashires heard whistles blowing down the trench system.

"Okay boys, fix bayonets!" shouted the officers.

John gave the photograph of dear Annie a kiss and put it back in his right breast pocket covering his heart. The infantrymen climbed up the ladders and over the top. John started to run in order to keep up with the rest of the platoon. He whispered to himself, "If I am going to kop it, I don't want to die alone." Suddenly the man next to him let out a scream as his arm was plucked neatly from its socket. The boys some two hundred yards in front of him started to fall like dominoes.

He heard the reassuring voice of Corporal Haslem, his Burnley accent coming across strongly, "Keep going lads. We will be into the bastards soon." The German trenches were some 400 yards away, and facing them was the Prussian 369 infantry division - highly trained and extremely well armed. John noticed that the barbed wire was still intact.

Suddenly he was in the wire, its cruel barbs cutting into his shins and knees. He tripped and fell on the wire, he looked ahead and could see the German troops firing, but also throwing these huge hand grenades. The noise and screams of those poor lads staring death in the face filled the air. John suddenly felt like he had been hit in the face by a sledgehammer. He instantly put his hands over his face, and on opening his eyes, noticed he could only see through one eye. In great pain he glanced down at his lap and could not comprehend the scene. His other eye lay on his knee.

"Oh Christ, I am practically blind!" As he looked to his left, all he could see through his remaining eye was pure carnage. There were piles of bodies of East Lancashire boys surrounding him, and the screams of men coming face to face with death. He heard voices above the sound of the intense gunfire and as he turned he could see a German soldier some feet away. His bayonet tip was dripping red with the blood of his mates. The Prussian infantryman shouted words John did not recognize.

"Shweinhundt!" he screamed. The bayonet attached to the enemy soldier's rifle was thrust deep in to John's chest entering him through his right breast pocket going through his cigarette packet and the wedding photograph of his beloved Annie, before reaching his heart. As the bayonet was withdrawn John let out a sigh, stared at the Sky in shock for a few seconds and slipped away.

Back in Whalley, Lancashire, Annie felt a shiver down her spine. She just knew that something was very wrong, she could not sleep that night, her stomach was in knots, and eating was impossible. She paced her kitchen floor, walked over Whalley nab, and sat in her chair staring in to space.

Four days later the postman arrived, and a letter hit her doormat. She rushed to the door, and immediately recognised John's handwriting. She also noticed a tear in the corner of the letter where the Sergeant Major's bayonet had spiked all the letters. She hurriedly opened the letter, her heart racing at great speed. A knot appeared in her throat and her eyes filled with tears as she read the letter. The words were deeply emotional.

"Dear Annie, you are the love of my life, I worship the very ground you walk on. If I cannot come back to you as myself, I will come back to you in the form of a ghost and say goodbye to you in the corner of the Western Gatehouse, our favourite place at Whalley Abbey."

She fell to the floor, heart broken, with tears racing down her cheeks. She asked herself why this war had to take her young husband who had no grudge with anyone. All he wanted was to grow old with his children and grandchildren. She walked across the village and down to the Western Gatehouse and sat in the corner of the 1330 ruin.

Suddenly she felt a presence and an aroma that she instantly recognized. She heard her name being called, and turned. There, some two feet away, surrounded by a warm bright glow was her beloved John. A huge warm smile on his face,

"Oh John!" she screamed, desperately trying to hug the glow, but her hands went straight through the apparition. John's ghost turned, smiled and blew her a kiss and ascended up through the Gatehouse roof and into the next world.

Young Annie knew that one day she would meet him again. She never married and in August 1977 she was reunited with him. The letter written from the Somme battlefield is still with Annie's family. As you read those brave words you notice some of the words have been smudged quite badly. Annie's granddaughter said it was her grandmother's tears that had distorted the ink.

Today the villagers living in Whalley talk about the ghosts of the Western Gatehouse, and John's name can be seen on the 14-18 cenotaph to this day. John Hesket, who was born at the wrong time of the last century. The Great War was the war to end all wars. Of course we all know different.

Chapter 7
Clitheroe Castle and its Ghostly Cavaliers

The King's soldiers entered Clitheroe, under the command of Captain Cuthbert, a ruthless man who would take anything he wanted, be it cattle, food or people. The vast majority of his men were foreign mercenaries, German or Dutch mercenaries paid by the King's purse. They occupied Clitheroe in 1643, and were hated by the locals. The Garrison had a nasty habit of stealing children from their parents for ransom money and if these parents did not cough up, then the children were cruelly murdered. The occupying troops also took girls who had just become women from their homes and they were systematically raped.

The residents of Clitheroe and district hoped and prayed that Oliver Cromwell and his Parliamentarian troops would liberate them soon from the barbarism that they had been subjected to in recent years.

Their hopes were raised on the 18th of August 1648 when the new model army arrived in the town. Cromwell, at the head, and Generals Lambert, Fairfax, and Assheton behind. He told Assheton, "You take Clitheroe. I will capture all the bridges over the River Ribble, and advance to the city of Preston."

General Assheton sent three infantry probes to take the castle and surrounding buildings. The defenders managed to repel all three attacks. The General was concerned about his losses and sent word back to the advancing column, requesting that they bring up the breaching canon. This canon was a huge weapon called "Humpty Dumpty" by the troops. The canon was charged and a salvo dispatched towards the Norman keep, with great effect, blowing a huge hole in the East wall of the keep.

Soon General Assheton's men heard cheering as the enemy raised the white flag from the keep's flag pole, and surrendered. The Church bells from nearby Saint

Mary's Church rang out at the celebration of Clitheroe's freedom from the occupying Royalists. A large group of prisoners were rounded up and placed in a make-shift prisoner of war camp situated in the Castle grounds. They knew that segregation would soon take place, some actually sold as mercenaries to the Venetian army and some sent to Bermuda, not to enjoy the sunshine, but to work in the sugar cane fields as slaves.

Three Royalist prisoners gathered together. Lieutenant Aitkin, Lieutenant Casewell and Captain Rockliffe.

"Let's make a break for it, when it gets dark!" They planned to escape at midnight, creep away in the darkness and get back to the King's forces. Under the cover of darkness, the three of them crawled out of the castle compound and into the town of Clitheroe. At first light they were a good four miles clear of the town, and then unwittingly walked straight into a Government patrol.

"Right!" shouted the Patrol Commander. "Escaped prisoners eh? You're going straight back into the Castle."

On arriving back in Clitheroe, General Assheton gave his commanders a stern ticking off for letting the three officers escape from the P.O.W cage. As a deterrent for any more escapes, he ordered the execution of all three officers in front of their fellow P.O.W's. A crude rostrum was built at the top of the stairs leading to the Keep's entrance. Each man had his hands tied behind his back and each man had to climb onto the rostrum and kneel down, placing their heads on the execution blocks.

Rockliffe, Aitken and Casewell bravely saluted their men who had been ordered to watch their deaths. Lieutenant Aitken shook the hands of his fellow officers, and knelt down. He then shouted "God save the King!"

With one swish of his axe the Executioner had whipped his head clean from the shoulders, making a sickening thud as Aitken's head bounced down the castle steps, stopping short of the watching prisoners.

Lieutenant Casewell was the next, he was not frightened to die, but did not want a painful death as he had a very short neck. His executioner would have to be very accurate to do the job properly. Casewell knelt down and also shouted, "God save the King!"

The executioner raised the axe, and brought it down. The axe came down catching Casewell across his shoulder bone. He screamed out in absolute agony. The axe was raised again, the second blow cutting into his spinal chord, but not killing the man. Casewell was in extreme pain and was horrified to find himself still alive. A voice shouted out, "Do it properly man!"

For the third time the axe was raised, coming down at great speed severing Casewell's head cleanly from his shoulders. Captain Rockliffe very bravely followed, also shouting, "God save the King!"

We are now going to turn the clock forward through the mists of time, and a bitterly cold January morning in 1982. A police squad car made its way up the drive to the Castle's courtyard. The purpose being to kill some time. Sergeant Bland looked at his watch, 2.35am.

"Four hours to go lads." He was on a routine patrol with two constables. The quiet town of Clitheroe was in a deep sleep.

"Let's go to the castle for a smoke break," he said. The police car parked up in the courtyard beneath the 800 year old Norman Keep.

"I'll keep the engine running lads, it's bitter out there," said the Sergeant. Constable Brennand handed out a Players Number Six to his fellow officers, the three of them inhaled deeply. Outside the wind howled around the Keep, there was some sleet in the air, and all three men looked forward to getting into bed at the end of their shift at 6.30am. They chatted about the usual topics; football, women and who they disliked the most in the constabulary.

All three of them considered themselves lucky as they were aware that Clitheroe and District was not a particularly lawless place, and as a result they had it quite cushy compared to neighbouring forces.

PC Brennand tapped his mate PC Gowling on the shoulder, "Hey lads, Did you hear that?"

"What?" replied Sergeant Bland.

"I thought I heard someone shout from the Castle."

"Not at this time of night, too late to find drunkards - also it's a Tuesday morning, not the sort of night you would expect to find someone up there," replied Bland. Above the sound of the engine and radiator they could clearly hear someone shout.

"That's definitely a voice!" said Gowling. Sounds like, "Save the King."

"It could be the wind Sarge," replied Brennand. For the third time a voice could be heard from the keep's battlements.

"That's definitely not wind lads, grab your torches we are going to have a look."

On opening the car doors, all three were met by a merciless icy wind that seemed to cut through their bodies. The three of them climbed the stone steps up to the keep, and inside, they shone their torches on the castle walls. The keep's roof had long gone, and was exposed to the elements. Driving rain and hail rained down on the policemen.

Suddenly PC Brennand let out a high pitched scream. Bland and Gowling turned round immediately, to see in the full beam of Brennand's torch a Royalist soldier advance and walk straight through the constable, shouting the words, "God save the King!"

The apparition walked through the wall and disappeared. Brennand's blood had froze, in shock Sergeant Bland shouted, "Let's get the hell out of here."

The three officers ran down the steps at a pace, jumped into the squad car and reversed straight into a horse trough, causing extensive damage to the vehicle. The car pulled up in the police station compound with severe damage to the right wing. The Inspector on seeing the three startled officers enter the police station knew instantly that there was indeed something seriously wrong from the look on their faces. The three officers were all soaking wet and ashen faced.

They turned as their Inspector demanded, "What is the problem Sergeant Bland?" For a few seconds the Sergeant could not seem to get any words out of his mouth. WPC Wilkes joked, "You three look as if you have just seen a ghost!"

"Right you three in my office now!" shouted the Inspector.

They informed him of their ghostly experience, and when they came back on duty that night, the three of them were the butt of many a joke from their fellow officers.

However one man did not laugh. The duty desk Sergeant. "Look lads, I believe you. I have been a bobby in Clitheroe for twenty five years and I too have seen the ghosts of Clitheroe castle."

Chapter 8
The Ghostly Night at Samlesbury Hall.

Samlesbury Hall, near Preston is a national treasure. It was built way back in 1322, and still standing in the 21st century. In the Hall's 800 year old history it has witnessed the execution of a priest, two murders, two suspicious deaths and a very sad suicide.

In the year 1923 the hall was in a terrible state of decay and in danger of falling down. Local builders gathered like a flock of vultures to take away the timber and stone to use in new buildings. At the 11th hour the Samlesbury Hall Preservation Society was formed, consisting of wealthy entrepreneurs and historians. They raised the necessary finance to save the ancient building, and their next job was to appoint someone whom they thought would be suitable to restore the Hall to its former glory.

One such man lived in Darwen, near Blackburn in Lancashire, Mr Michael Palin (no relation to the Monty Python star). He was a highly skilled expert on medieval buildings, and had worked on Bramhall in Cheshire, Leven's Hall, Westmorland, and Smithills, Bolton to name just a few.

Michael arrived at Samlesbury on a beautiful June morning in 1923 with his four apprentices. He allocated various rooms for his boys to work on, and would check their progress throughout the day. Michael took his ladder into the reception area, and placed it against the wall. He noticed the wall was under great pressure and would have to be rebuilt as it was almost concave. He climbed the ladder and with a hammer and chisel started to knock out a large lintel stone that was badly eroded. With a huge heave, he got the lintel out and let it fall to the ground.

To his horror, at the foot of the ladder stood a little boy with curly black hair just staring up at Palin. The lintel stone fell earthwards at speed. Palin shouted, "Look out!"

The boy did not move. The lintel missed his head by a fraction, actually grazing the boy's nose.

Palin came down the ladder at great speed to give this boy a piece of his mind; he could have been killed. But the role was completely reversed, and the little boy, with an aggressive look on his face shouted at Palin. "Mr Bradyll won't like this! You have no right to do this!" The boy pointed to an oil painting on the opposite wall of Mr Gail John Bradyll, the second owner of Samlesbury Hall.

Palin told the lad, "Now I have every right to be here. I have been appointed by the new owners to repair the Hall. You stand back, you could have been killed by the lintel." Palin climbed back up the ladder, and asked the boy, "Where have you come from?" He was under the impression that there was just him and his four apprentices in the Hall.

Palin glanced back at the cavity he had made by removing the eroded stone, and then glanced back in the direction of the little boy. The boy was nowhere to be seen. "That's strange," muttered Palin. "He must be a very quick runner."

Summer turned to winter and the old Hall was beginning to look like its old self again. New timber tiles and floor boards had been installed. They arrived on a bitterly cold December morning for another day of hard graft. Michael was very pleased with his lads' work. They were now all working in the reception area adjacent the chapel.

Suddenly, outside the weather changed. The blue sky disappeared and was replaced by huge white clouds full of snow. A wind whipped up, and heavy snow came down from the heavens. In a short period the snow lay deep and thick, not only on the Hall's lawns but on the road adjacent the building.

"I am sorry lads," said Michael, "There is no way we will get back to Darwen tonight. The roads are unserviceable. There is no way the horse and cart will get down the road, We will have to spend the night here."

The apprentices complained, but Palin shouted, "Lads, let's go into the forest, grab what wood we can and stock pile the fire in the reception room." They came back from the forest with branches and twigs and soon had a huge glowing fire in the reception room. It was soon nightfall, and the apprentices got blankets from various rooms and also some cushions, and made themselves as comfortable as possible to settle down for a very long night.

In those days, there were no Nintendo's, mobile phones, TV or radio. The only entertainment was indeed a good sleep. The four apprentices fell into a reasonably comfortable sleep. Michael threw some more wood on the fire and then rolled out his bed role. For a few minutes he gazed into the fire, then turned over to settle down for the night. Outside the snow fell heavily and a strong wind howled across the roof.

Michael turned over and in the corner of his eye he could make out a golden glow from the chapel door entrance, situated in the corner of the reception room. At first he thought that it was the reflection from the fire, but the glow became brighter and then suddenly formed the shape of a woman. Palin's heart-beat increased and he inhaled in spasms, as his eyes took in the shape of a very beautiful young women in Tudor dress. She elegantly glided past Palin and in between the sleeping apprentices, and knelt in front of the roaring fire. She clasped her hands together in prayer, Palin from his vantage point heard her whisper a prayer, "I pray my husband will return safely to me." She then vaporized, leaving a very sweet sugary scent in the air.

Palin rubbed his eyes and shook his head, "Am I dreaming?" He touched his toes and slapped his thigh. "I am awake!" he muttered. Then, once again to his right, he noticed yet another glowing bright light. Palin thought about waking all his apprentices and ordering them to leave the hall, but out of the second bright glowing light appeared a man in military uniform from the civil war period. The figure had a goatee beard, bandoliers across his chest, feathers in his hat, a sword by his side and was wearing riding boots. This apparition frightened Palin a lot more that the beautiful Tudor woman he had witnessed minutes earlier.

Frozen to his bed role, Palin watched the ghost move to the fireplace as if he was the only person there. He heard the words, "I hope I survive the war." With a crackle in the air the ghostly cavalier melted into thin air, filling the room with a strong aroma of leather.

By this time Palin was in a state of shock and dismay, he did not know how to react. He considered whether he should wake the lads up. He went across to the window, and noticed in the light from the fire, that the blizzard outside was getting more ferocious. More heavy snow came down from the heavens.

He sighed, "We are practically prisoners here." Something caught his eye, he glanced towards the chapel door and to his horror another light appeared - this time much smaller than the last two. This light materialised into the little boy with the curly black hair who in June of that year, had stood at the bottom of the ladder when Palin had removed the lintel and had been horrified to watch the stone fall earthwards towards the lad's head. The boy ran across the room like the other two ghosts. He was unaware that he was being watched. Palin witnessed the boy running straight through his four apprentices.

All four of them had managed to sleep whilst this paranormal activity had taken place all around them. Well, you could imagine Michael did not sleep well for the rest of that night, but most surprisingly when his four boys woke up he did not tell them about his ghostly encounter.

In fact on getting home to Darwen, he never told his wife and four daughters. This was his secret, but some twenty years later, as an elderly gentleman on a bright summer's day, he walked past Samlesbury Hall.

As he had on many occasions, he liked to visit to admire his work on the old building. He noticed parked just outside the main entrance a military vehicle belonging to the Royal Air Force.

"RAF! What are they doing there?" he asked himself. He walked across the neatly mowed lawns to the reception door, as he opened the door he noticed two people in RAF uniform, one male the other female. Both of them were admiring the oil painting of Mr Gail Bradyll, the second owner of the Hall.

As the door clicked open, the two RAF personnel turned round. Michael's eyes made immediate contact with the young lady in the RAF uniform and for a few seconds, he just stared at her. You can imagine she felt very embarrassed by Michael's actions.

The RAF officer intervened, "May we help you?" he said. Michael sighed. He recognised her as being the same beautiful young woman he had seen walk out of the golden bright light in the Tudor dress twenty years earlier. Palin introduced himself, and told her of his experience, those twenty years ago.

She burst into tears, "Mr Palin, I do not disbelieve a word you have said, but I am from the city of London. I have never been to Lancashire before. But as we drove past in the staff car, I shouted, 'Stop! Stop! I know this place. I have been here before', and you Mr Palin have answered all my anxieties."

Chapter 9
Murder in Blackburn 1875

On the 14th of May 1875, nine year old Emily Welland was walking home with her two older brothers. They made their way past the Wheatsheaf Hotel in the town centre. The two boys were walking slightly ahead, and as they made their way past the hotel, Emily seemed to vanish. Some 100 yards up the road, the two brothers turned round expecting to see their sister. Both lads were extremely surprised when they noticed she had literally disappeared. "She must have somehow got past us and sprinted home."

On arriving back home, both lads were horrified to find that their sister was not at home. Their mother screamed at them, "Why did you let her out of your sight?" The boys tried to explain, "She just vanished mother, into thin air!"

Mother and her two sons ran back into town shouting for young Emily. They retraced their steps, but it was to no avail. Emily had completely disappeared. Her mother was understandably distressed and ran into the town's police station to report her daughter's disappearance. Inspectors Potts and Eastwood organised two search parties for both areas that Emily had been on that day. Sadly both search parties drew a blank. Emily's mother and father were both deeply affected and for the next seven days experienced terrible trauma and stress.

A Mr Peter Fairclough of Waddington took his dog for a walk in the local park, his labrador came out of the undergrowth with some newspaper in its mouth saturated in blood. Fairclough grabbed the newspaper and tore it out of the creature's mouth. To Fairclough's horror, a child's severed hand fell onto the park pathway. He made immediate contact with the authorities and Blackburn police arrived in the form of Potts and Eastwood and a constable named Livesey.

"Right, Gentlemen! Let's search the rest of the undergrowth." In a matter of minutes, PC Livesey had found some more newspaper that was soaked in blood and also sadly containing a child's limb.

Inspector Eastwood informed his colleagues, "Gentlemen. From looking at both organs I am sure you will agree they belong to an infant and we can only presume that the organs are from Emily's body. I shall inform her parents."

A day later, a Mrs Turner from Bastwell, North Blackburn, made her way to her work as a weaver in a local mill. In the semi light, she tripped over some newspapers, again saturated in blood. On picking up the newspapers she noticed that they had been used to wrap something quite heavy. As she opened the package, to her horror they contained a child's torso. She was violently sick, and after being comforted by passers by, Blackburn police were once again informed. Eastwood and Potts took the organs to the police mortuary. There the two officers inspected the newspapers and indeed the child's torso. Eastwood noticed wrapped up in the paper was quite a considerable amount of human hair, but different coloured hair, belonging to different people.

"I have it!" shouted Inspector Eastwood. Whoever committed this dastardly crime committed it in a barbers shop."

"My God, you're probably right!" said Potts.

Their next job was to visit every barbers shop in Blackburn, all thirty two. They made a routine visit to all of them, including Mr William Dace. He was twenty five years old, married and had two daughters and gave the impression of being respectable. Inspector Potts noticed a huge pile of Lancashire telegraph newspapers on the shelf inside his shop. Potts had his notebook with him and he had taken down all the numbers and dates on the telegraph newspaper used to wrap the poor girl's organs in.

"Mr Dace, can I ask you please, where are the first two weeks of May's Telegraph newspapers?"

For a few seconds Dace looked nervously around him, and then with a look of pure innocence he said, "Oh, I used them to light the fire."

This answer seemed to satisfy both officers and they left the premises and made their way back to Blackburn police station. On the way there, both officers were concerned to see newspaper bill boards criticising Blackburn police. Words like "Local police incompetent" and "a month gone and no arrests."

Both men entered their office, and were informed that if they did not get results soon, Blackburn police would be a laughing stock. The murder shocked the locals, and as a result children were escorted by their parents to and from school. As each day passed, the billboards became more insulting. The Home Office in London showed some concern as this story had hit the national press front pages. A local cotton baron called John Stalwart offered one hundred pounds to anyone who could successfully catch this evil child murderer. The home office also put up one hundred pounds for the arrest of this maniac. £200 pounds in 1875 was indeed a huge amount of money.

Who should pick up the gauntlet but a thirteen year old boy from Preston called Peter Levine. He wrote to Inspector Potts, "Sir, I have a little dog called Morgan. He has a marvellous sense of smell he will find your murderer."

Potts, Eastwood and PC Livesey all laughed at the letter. Their laughing stopped as they looked out of the window at the new billboards across the street, adjacent to the police station. The words read, "Blackburn detectives no nearer to catching child murderer. They are over paid and under worked!"

Eastwood glanced at young Peter's letter. "Sir, let's bring this young lad in from Preston. We have to explore every avenue."

Two days later at the town's railway station Potts

and Eastwood met Peter Levine with his little dog Morgan on the platform. Morgan was a collie lurcher cross, and shivered with fright when the two officers tried to stroke it.

"Sir, can we please go to the mortuary? Morgan will get a scent from the newspapers used to wrap the victims organs in," requested Peter.

They made their way to the mortuary and Potts opened the cold room door and removed Emily's remains from the shelf inside.

"Come on boy!" said Peter, nudging the dog towards the bloodied newspaper. Morgan started barking and ran straight to the door. Peter's eyes lit up. "Sir, he has the scent!" he shouted excitedly. "Please open the door!"

The crossbreed ran straight onto King Street, onto Jubilee Street, followed at quite a pace by Potts, Eastwood, Livesey and young Peter.

Morgan turned and ran onto Darwen Street, stopping outside William Dace's barber shop. Behind the frosted glass of the barber shop's front door was a very frosty faced William Dace. Morgan scratched at the door as the police officers and Peter gathered outside the shop. "Sir, Morgan has a scent. It's coming from inside this shop Sir!" said Peter, with a look of exuberance on his face.

Eastwood hammered on the door. Dace opened it and Morgan ran straight through his legs and started barking. The dog sniffed the carpet and then advanced towards the fireplace, barking continuously.

Peter shouted, "Sir, he knows there is something up the fireplace chimney!"

Inspector Eastwood knelt down and reached up behind the chimney breast and found something lodged in a recess. He grabbed what felt like a package, and pulled out some more newspaper. As he opened the package, he stared at poor Emily's charred skull.

"Right, arrest this man!"

Dace was pushed against the wall, handcuffed and then given a good hiding by PC Livesey. At last they had got their man. Dace was sent for trial at Liverpool and admitted to the murder.

He said that he had been drinking very heavily at the Wheatsheaf Hotel, and as he was about to leave he leaned against a marble pillar near the doorway. As Emily walked past he grabbed her, he noticed that there was no one in the hotel alley way, and placing his hand over her mouth he picked her up and took her the forty yards to the stable block at the back of the Wheatsheaf. He threw the girl on the straw and committed a serious sexual offence on her. He then made the decision to murder her, as he was aware that she would obviously inform on him. He then cruelly strangled her. He took his coat off and wrapped her body in the coat. He then took her corpse back to his barber shop and dissected the body. And it was indeed the fact that he did not get rid of the body parts very well that led to his conviction. Dace was to hang for his crime.

Young Peter Levine was invited to Blackburn town hall to attend a civic reception. He was delighted when the Mayor awarded him the reward of a £200 cheque.

Sadly Peter never saw a penny as his mother and father spent every penny by the time he was eighteen years old.

In the 1960's parts of old Blackburn were just bulldozed away and with it some beautiful old buildings were lost forever. But the Old Wheatsheaf Hotel is still there as a listed building. The hotel is now called the Stage Door, but the marble pillars where Dace waited to commit his evil crime are still there. And so are the stables at the back of the hotel. Over the years there have been stories of guests who have been woken by the sound of sobbing and screams coming from the stable block where poor Emily's life was taken from her all those years ago. In 1955 the police were called as a guest was convinced that a murder was taking place in the stables. As for Dace he became the first Lancastrian ever to be a Madame Tussauds wax work dummy and was known simply as, "the Blackburn Butcher."

Chapter 10
Stoneyhurst and its Ghostly Revenge

Stoneyhurst College is a private school, and has been referred to as the Eton of the North. Certainly the college has the same standard of education as you will find at Eton, and a similar tuition fee for its students. The only difference from Eton is all Stoneyhurst students are ardent Catholics and as a result the college is open to Catholics from around the globe

The school boasts, 3 Saints, 7 Archbishops, 7 Victoria Cross winners, and some very famous old boys, in particular JR Tolkien, Sir Arthur Conan Doyle, Sir Charles Laughton to name only a few. You can start your education at the age of four and leave when you're eighteen.

In the days when Britain had an empire, it was quite common for tea plantation owners to leave their children at the college at the age of four and say, "Goodbye, see you when you're eighteen."

Let's turn the clock back in time to 1936. Every school has popular pupils, they usually come in the form of sporting heroes, or in some cases brilliant academics. That year, two boys caught the admiration of not only fellow pupils but teachers as well. Both boys had charisma and had a keen determination to beat each other on the running track, on the rugby and cricket fields, and also in class. One boy being Kevin Burne from the English Lake District. His parents were the proud owners of Colton Hall and the huge estate that went with it. Kevin had indeed been born with a silver spoon in his mouth, and as the only child, one day he would inherit the Hall, and his father's huge estate.

The other lad, young Hurbst had leadership skills and was literally frightened of no-one. This included teachers and fellow students. At Stoneyhurst, he was not a bully, but nobody would dare to pick a fight with him or complain about him. In the spring of 1936 however, he did come into contact with a new boy that did challenge his popularity.

Gerhardt Hurbst, came from Lubeck in Germany. His family came from a very strong Catholic background, and were millionaires. They had made their wealth in a similar fashion to the Burnes family had in the Lake District. They owned huge tracts of land and factories. Hurbst, on arriving at the college - had amazed his fellow students with his immaculate use of the English language and also his speed on the running track.

Naturally, Hurbst's popularity caused friction with Burne, and one lunch time, Hurbst challenged Burne to a race, a 100 yards challenge.

Burne accepted, in his clipped upper class accent, "I'll show this Hun how it's done what." The teachers heard about the challenge and as a result the whole school was invited to watch these two compete in the challenge. Both athletes made their way to the starting line, and knelt in their positions.

For a second they glanced at each other, Burne smiling at Hurbst, "Well old chap, you're going to lose this one I'm afraid!"

Hurbst's reply was, "No, it is you who will lose and tomorrow I shall also beat you in algebra and Latin, my family's honour is at stake."

The sports teacher placed a blank round in to the starting pistol. "Ready Gentlemen, on your marks, get set, go!" Both lads started perfectly, sprinting at Olympic qualifying speed.

The finishing line was nearly upon them when Burne felt a sharp pain in his running shoe, a spike had come up from the sole, four feet from the finishing line. There was a huge roar from the German boy's house members as Hurbst edged over the line. Burne was gasping for breath as he took his running shoe off.

"The blasted spike came through!" he shouted.

Hurbst shouted out loud so all around him could hear, "Burne, you are a bad loser, your excuse is pathetic, you are a bad loser."

The blood in Burnes' body started to boil, and he nudged forward and grabbed Hurbst's collar.

"Get your hands off me!" demanded Hurbst.

"Right let's have this out. A boxing match will settle this!" said Burne.

Two teachers intervened, "Stop this disgusting behaviour gentlemen now!"

"Sir," shouted Burne. "I challenge Hurbst to a boxing match in the school gym this Saturday afternoon."

The headmaster was informed, he said, "Well, we are a Catholic College, we teach all our pupils to love thy brother," he said, "But we also produce some of the finest officers in the British and Commonwealth Empire. Yes I sanction the match, to four rounds each."

The next four days were very tense not only for Burne and Hurbst, but for the opposing houses. Both had to give support to their own house representative. Classes were disrupted as both boys had the same lessons in Latin, mathematics and geography. In these subjects, both students achieved maximum marks and could not be separated in their mastery of their chosen subjects.

Finally Saturday afternoon arrived, and the school's gymnasium was filled to the gunnels. There was a huge cheer as both boys entered the ring.

The referee, shouted, "I want a good clean fight, no biting, kicking or below the belt blows. On the bell engage."

Both boys were seventeen years old and had the physique of men. Hurbst seemed to glide and skip around his opponent, and caught Burne cleanly with an uppercut. Burne fell onto the canvas with blood squirting from his lip.

The referee was about to count him out when Burne shouted, "No, I am alright!" He got to his feet, and was immediately caught again by Hurbst's mastery of footwork, and landed yet another perfect uppercut. Burne hit the canvas again, this time to his horror the referee counted him out. For Burne and his supporters this was a

65

huge shock, this was their hero who had not only been beaten on the running track, but now also in the boxing ring. The referee insisted that both men shake each other's hand.

Burne being an English gentleman swallowed his pride and said, "Well played Hurbst."

To Burne's surprise, the German turned, looked burn in the eye and said, "You are a loser and one day I will be the death of you," he said with a sarcastic smile. Those words shocked Burne almost as if he had ice cubes in his bloodstream.

Hurbst was deadly serious, for the rest of that term both boys were separated in lessons and indeed sports.

In the Summer of 1939 they both left Stoneyhurst College. Kevin Burne returned to his native Grassmere and the family estate. Hurbst to his father's huge industrial empire. In September 1939 Great Britain declared war on Nazi Germany, and nineteen year old Kevin Burne entered the Naval Academy at Dartmouth for officer training. As was expected he came top of all his lessons and indeed was commissioned, and posted to HMS Prince of Wales.

Two years later he witnessed the shocking sinking of HMS Hood as both battleships engaged the German Pocket battleship's Bismarck and Prince Augen. After this engagement and the huge loss of the Hood's crew, Burne began to grow a hatred for the Germans. Memories came flooding back of Guhart Hurbst and his attitude at Stoneyhurst. Burne was delighted when the British battleship King George the Fifth sank the Bismark.

In 1943 he was promoted to Captain of the Corvette HMS Bantree and became a Convoy Escort. Again he witnessed some horrific sinkings from U boat attacks, and had seen many an oil tanker erupt in flame, while their brave crews were still on board.

HMS Bantree was a happy ship and Burne, despite being just twenty one years old, had the head of a much older man. The U boats had taken the lives of many of his friends, not only Royal Navy but merchantmen too. Some of his crew had also been torpedoed on other warships, losing mates. Aboard the Bantree was a feverish determination of hunting and sinking a U Boat.

In November 1944, the Corvette was escorting convoy LZ42. Captain Burne was on the bridge, "Contact green zero – two, Sir!" shouted an excited crew-member up the voice pipe. Action stations were sounded and the gun crews closed up. In the asdic room, the pinging sound of the contact became more frequent.

"Steer port!" shouted Burne. He had no idea, but some feet beneath the Bantree was indeed Gurhart Hurbst, Commander of the U86.

"Damn!" shouted Hurbst, "they have a contact! Be quiet men, we shall dive to deeper water." Hurbst had been here before and his men had the utmost confidence in him. The U86 had sunk many allied vessels and Hurbst had six months previously been awarded the Iron Cross from Admiral Donitz himself.

Out of his flotilla of 1942, he was the only survivor, and his men regarded him as a very clever fox, eluding the Royal Navy on many occasions. They also knew him to be quite ruthless, not only with the enemy but also with his own crew. If he felt men under his command to be weak he had them ejected immediately. The U86 had a wolf painted on the conning tower, and on coming home to port other crews called her the Lone Wolf.

In 1943, in the Mediterranean, she had inflicted huge losses on allied shipping, but had also committed war crimes on survivors in life boats by ordering his men to open fire on the defenceless sailors.

One or two of his fellow officers had complained to the Kreigsemarine Admirals, and he was going to be court marshalled, but he said, "It is our duty to win this war, and if these men had got to another ship they would take up arms against us again." Adolf Hitler had personally stopped the court marshall.

Hms Bantree closed in on the enemy submarine, the asdic operator shouted, "We are on top of her Sir! I think she is diving into deeper water."

"Prepare to depth charge," shouted Burne.

Bantree released four depth charges. The first explosion turned all the lights out on the U boat for a few seconds, and a huge shock wave reverberated along the hull. The second explosion cut a deep hole in her side. Hurbst shouted, "Prepare to surface!" The U boat was taking in water but she had sufficient air in her tanks to get to the surface.

The lookout next to Burne on the Bantree shouted, "Look Sir, she is surfacing!"

"Right. Bring her about coxen. We will bloody ram the bastard. Full steam ahead!" cried Burne.

The gun crews were ordered to open fire and the forward gun opened fire, and was joined by the Oilekon anti aircraft gun. A huge spout of water could be seen near the U boat. Burne looked through his glasses and noted the wolf painting on the conning tower.

Inside the U boat, armour piercing bullets from the Oilikon were ricocheting inside the hull. Hurbst to his shock, was hit in the throat by one of the bullets and his mouth filled with blood. Speech was made impossible, so he made hand gestures to his crew to get out. Although weak from blood loss, he managed to see some of his crew climb the conning tower to escape.

The Bantree was closing in for the kill, at maximum speed. She rammed the U boat on the surface, crippling her. The German boat immediately capsized, rolled over and sank.

Burne and his crew cheered. They had made a significant contribution to the war effort and many of them felt no concern for the U boat's crew, mainly because they had seen many of their mates die over the past few years.

HMS Bantree made her way into Liverpool, her crew acknowledging the cheers from other royal naval vessels and port staff. On docking, a naval jeep arrived with the top brass, and on walking down the gangway – Burne saluted and received a huge smile back from Admiral Cunningham.

"Well done Captain Burne!" He said as he shook the captain's hand. "Naval intelligence have been tracking that bastard for some time. The U86 has claimed thousands of tons of shipping but also the lives of many a good rating. The commander Gehart Hurbst was known as the Lone Wolf."

Burne shuddered in surprise.

"Excuse me, Sir," said Burne, "could you repeat that name again?"

"Gerhart Hurbst."

"I know this man, Sir. I went to Stoneyhurst College with him before the war." For a few seconds Burne stared into space. He remembered those chilling words from Hurbst, *"One day I will take your life!"*

As it happened, Burne had done just that. That night, the crew of the Bantree celebrated in the city of Liverpool, and in due course their Captain was not only mentioned in dispatches but also decorated. Deep inside, Burne felt some relief that Hurbst was indeed dead, as his words at Stoneyhurst had chilled him to the bone.

At the end of hostilities, Burne returned to the Lake District and the only water he sailed on again was the calm waters of Grassmere.

In the Summer of 1965, he sat down at the breakfast table and as usual read the daily newspaper. Something caught his eye in the press, "U boat found off Southern Ireland, with a wolf painted on conning tower, Believed to be U86 sunk by HMS Bantree in 1944."

Burne was naturally fascinated by the find. He was also extremely interested to learn that an Irish businessman was offering diving services on the wreck. Burne looked up from his newspaper, "I have to go and look at that wreck."

His curiosity had won the day. He rushed upstairs

and started packing.

His dear wife shouted, "Kevin, what's the rush?"

"I have to go!" he shouted while throwing shirts, pyjamas and socks into the suitcase.

"Why now?" she enquired.

"I just have to go!"

As if it was his destiny, he ran downstairs, ordered a taxi to Oxenholme station and a ticket for Liverpool. From the city he caught the ferry to the Republic of Ireland. The salt spray in the air brought back memories of the Bantree.

On arriving in Ireland he again purchased another ticket to the west coast, and booked in to a bed and breakfast. He had brought with him the newspaper and indeed the address of the Irish businessman who was conducting the dives to the U86.

The following day he telephoned a Mr Eddie Quade. He informed him that he would take him personally to the wreck and also provide the necessary equipment for the dive. The following morning Kevin woke up, got out of bed, and had a strange feeling about the day. For a minute or two he asked himself, "What am I doing here? Why am I doing this?" He shrugged his shoulders, got dressed and after breakfast met Mr Quade.

"Good morning Mr Burne. I have everything ready for you Sir, including the latest aqualung wet suit," he said it in a strong Irish accent.

"How far out is the wreck?" enquired Kevin.

"Two miles out, in deep water, but not deep enough to stop us having ten minutes on the wreck," said Quade.

"Have you ever been inside the U-boat?"

"No, but I am convinced that there are some compartments that have not been opened since the sinking."

"Have you taken many divers to the wreck?" enquired Burne.

"Oh yes," he replied, "but today there is just you

and me." They boarded the converted fishing vessel that would take them to the wreck. They set out into the ocean. A short time later they came across a buoy.

"That's the site of the wreck!" said Quade. Both men tested their aqualungs and goggles and carefully put their flippers on.

"Right Mr Burne, please follow me."

Both men fell backwards into the deep Atlantic Ocean. Quade ushered Burne to use the chain attached to the buoy to take him down to the wreck. Burne pulled on the chain, with each pull taking him deeper under water. The pressure was felt after thirty feet, and there was another thirty to go before the U86 came into view. Quade had with him a very powerful underwater light not to dissimilar to a searchlight.

Suddenly the conning tower of the submarine became visible, along with the lone wolf insignia painted on its side. Burne breathed heavily into his mask, his heart beat raised as he took in the scene before him. He noticed the huge hole in the side of the submarine where HMS Bantree had rammed her. He swam to the hole and turned to Quade, hand gesturing that he shine his light into the wreck. Quade pointed to his watch indicating that they had only enough oxygen to stay for ten more minutes.

Burne grabbed the light and put it inside the sub. He followed inside, where he noticed some watertight doors still closed in the section he had just entered. He made his way to one of the doors. Burne had no idea that outside the submarine, Quade was getting very agitated, he had never been inside the wreck and he had certainly never seen any of the other divers enter the wreck. Quade again looked at his watch.

"My God, we have to go, our air supply has only six minutes left!" Quade made his way to the hole were Burne had entered, to inform him by hand signals of the danger they were in. As he poked his head into the wreck, he was met by a huge release of air. In his shock he got out of the wreck and made his way to the surface at great speed, with two minutes oxygen left in his tank he got to the surface.

He took his mask off and as he clambered on board the fishing vessel he shouted, "The bloody idiot! Why has he gone inside?"

Sixty feet beneath him, Kevin Burne was indeed fighting for his life. On entering the submarine wreck, he had managed to prise open one of the water-tight doors. With a whoosh of escaped air, he found to his horror that he was surrounded by swirling skeletons, some with life preservers still on. The room filled with sea water in an instant. Burne turned round and swam back to the opening that would take him back to the surface. He shone the bright light in front of him. The current inside the sub had moved all the skeletons to the area were he had entered the U boat and somehow had filled the opening due to the current. He felt dizzy and realised his oxygen was indeed running out. He grabbed at the nearest skeleton, tugging at bones furiously. He had to get out and back to the surface. In panic and desperation, he pulled at the skeletons as his life literally depended on it. He noticed that there was just one barring his exit from the U-boat. In the beam of his light he could see around the neck of this skeleton was the iron cross. Burne screamed, as he realized that he was looking at Gerhart Hurbst's skeleton.

In a last effort he tried to push the skeleton away from the opening. The skeleton was lodged across the escape hole, but he knew he was too late. Burne's oxygen had indeed run out.

As Burne gasped in horror in his last seconds of life, he looked at Hurbst's skeletal face which seemed to laugh at him.

"One day I will take your life."

Chapter 11
Peg O'Nell

On the banks of the River Ribble in the old West Riding of Yorkshire stands a beautiful old hall called Waddow hall. The hall belonged to a textile baron called John Stark, a very wealthy chap. He owned the huge textile factory called Primrose Mill in the year 1797. Stark was married but was certainly not the best of husbands, and had taken his pleasure with many young ladies in the region. He would make the long journey to the city of Liverpool to watch the ships come in from the southern states of America, and would go to the merchant halls and to buy cotton by the bale and have it sent to his factory in the West Riding.

One autumn day he made his way to the merchant hall and his eye was attracted by a rather beautiful young lady. Her name was Peg O'Nell from county Wicklow in Southern Ireland. She was seventeen and came from a large family, her mission in Liverpool was to look for work. She had the misfortune of meeting Stark.

"Looking for work are you?" he enquired.

"Yes Sir I am," she replied.

"Well young lady, your luck is in, I shall offer you employment at my residence as a maid." Young Peg excitedly accepted her new employers kind offer. She had no idea but she was in serious danger. She climbed into Stark's coach and they set off for Waddow Hall.

On arriving, Starks wife shouted, "Who is she?"

"Well," said Stark, "she is our new maid."

"But we don't need any more servants, we have too many as it is," shouted Mrs Stark. Poor Peg felt very insecure by the cold steely look that Mrs Stark had on her face. Peg was ushered into the house and was introduced to Vickery, the head Butler. He was known to be a rather devious man.

"Come this way," he said, taking her up three flights

of stairs. "This is your bed," he announced, pointing to a room with six beds. "All the maids sleep in here."

Peg was woken at 5.00am the following morning and put to work in the kitchens. After breakfast she took coal to the living room to stoke up the fire.

As she entered the room, she noticed Mr Stark sitting in a chair by the window, reading. "Ah Peg. How are you settling in dear?" he asked as he got up and walked towards Peggy. He gently took both of her hands in his, in a warm gesture, and looked her in the eye.

"Peggy, if you need anything just ask, my dear." He said with a glint in his eye. "I will look after you."

Stark had two sons, called James and Ian, both of the lads were in their early teens. As they came downstairs for breakfast, they sat at the table. Peg came into the room with some warm breakfast plates. Both boys on seeing her enter the room, looked at her in silence. Their jaws dropped as they took in this beautiful young woman's elegant feminine features.

Ian gently elbowed James, and whispered, "She is simply divine."

Both lads surrendered their hearts to this truly beautiful young woman. Mrs Stark looked up from her breakfast plate, with a huge frown on her face. She couldn't escape the fact that, not only were her sons blatantly falling in love with young Peg, but also her husband was too. Vickery the butler was also aware of the situation. He had two daughters, Isabel and Jane and he wanted both girls to marry the two Stark sons to secure their futures. Like Mrs Stark, he also viewed young Peggy with distaste, and with a deep concern for the future of his daughters.

Two days later John Stark made his way up to the servants' quarters. He had consumed a large quantity of rum, He knocked on the maids room.

"Just a minute," a voice called back. The head maid opened the door.

"Yes Sir, Can I help you?"

"Could I please have a word with young Peg please?" he asked.

"Well Sir, she is asleep."

"Please wake her!" He demanded. The head maid shook Peggy's shoulder.

"Wake up Peg, the master wants to talk to you. Get up now!" she demanded. In a state of semi-sleep, Peggy made her way to the door where stark was waiting.

"Please Peggy, I need to talk to you." He gestured her down the stairs, to the living room. In the living room Stark could not help himself. He wrapped his arms around the girl, and hugged her closely. His emotions had beaten him, he had fallen in love with young Peg. For a minute or two he stared at her, his eyes taking in her beautiful face.

"Would you like a drink my dear?"

"Thank you Sir," she said in a soft confused voice. He poured her a large Jamaican rum. Peg was seventeen years old, and in Wicklow she had seen her father and brothers drink hard liqueur. She was no stranger to alcohol. She gulped the rum down, Stark filled her glass again and in a short time the glass had been charged three more times. She felt relaxed for the first time since she had left Ireland. Stark slowly hugged and squeezed the girl again, he became sexually excited, and pressed himself against her. She laughed out loudly, as the rum took effect.

Stark carefully pulled her nightdress off her shoulders and dropped it onto the floor, leaving Peg completely naked. She stood close to the fire. Her curvaceous body beautifully silhouetted in the light from the fire. Stark could not take his eyes off her. He had never seen such a wonderful female body. He threw his jacket on the carpet, his shoes and trousers quickly followed, his heart hammered in his chest. Stark carefully took her by the shoulders and gently pulled her to the floor. The effect of the rum affected Peggy's vision, and indeed any attempt to resist. She felt him enter her, she let out a slight scream as he took her. Stark let out a deep sigh as he felt he had just entered heaven.

Whilst this act was taking place, Mrs Stark heard noises coming from the living room. She shouted for the butler Vickery. The pair of them made their way to the source of all the noise. As Mrs Stark entered the room, there on the floor before her lay her husband and young Peg. John Stark was in the final seconds of completing his love making, but a second before he was about to climax, his wife had brought down the fire poker handle on the back of his head, taking him from ecstasy to agony in an instant.

"Get up, get up!" screamed Mrs Stark.

Vickery shouted also, "Right young woman, get upstairs now!" throwing her nighty at her.

"You swine!" shouted Mrs Stark. "How could you, in our own home?"

Stark had no excuse. He pulled his pants back on and poured himself another rum. The back of his head was bleeding quite badly, from being struck with the poker. He tried to make an excuse, but his wife had heard it all before.

In the meantime Peg had been thrown onto her bed by Vickery. "Right, lass – you're in deep bloody trouble! You will be out by tomorrow, back to bloody Ireland!"

Peg sighed. She brushed her hair back with her hand and made her way to the sink to regurgitate the rum. She was up by 5 'o'clock the following morning, nursing a very bad headache due to the rum consumed the night previous.

She came downstairs with the other maids, and there at the bottom of the stairs stood James and Ian, the two Stark boys.

"Good morning Peggy!" said both lads, wearing a trance-like look on their faces.

Then came the full horror of Mrs Stark and Vickery, "Come this way!" shouted Mrs Stark, in an aggressive manner. Peg was led into the reception room and told to sit down.

Mrs Stark shouted, "Right young woman, you are leaving. Pack all your belonging and Vickery will take you to the railway station."

Peg made her way upstairs crying, "This job has been a nightmare, I don't have any affection for Mr Stark or his sons. I have been basically raped by him." She muttered to herself as she followed her orders. Once she had packed her suitcase, she made her way down the stairs.

Suddenly John Stark appeared. "Peg! What's wrong?" he asked, looking terribly concerned.

"I have been sacked as a result of last night's actions" she muttered, in a sarcastic voice.

"You're not going!" shouted Stark.

His two sons came running into the room "Peggy, please don't go, We love you!" shouted the boys.

Vickery shouted,"Sir, with respect - Mrs Stark has just sacked her. She is leaving this morning."

With an agitated look on his face, Stark said, "She is not going, anywhere! Peg - go back to your room and unpack!"

"Sir, I protest!" shouted Vickery.

"I run this house, Mr Vickery - go back to your duties immediately man!"

Well, Peggy made her way back to her room, wishing that she was indeed going to the railway station and back home.

Mrs Stark shouted at her husband. "She has to go!"

"No, she has not!" shouted John, "I run this house and you will obey me!" he shouted back at his wife.

She stormed out of the room and shouted for Vickery. "Right. Vickery, I have a plan."

The two of them made their way out onto the huge garden in front of the hall.

"Tonight we shall deal our own justice," said Mrs Stark, and they made their plans together. In the early hours of the morning they tip-toed up the stairs to the maids' room.

All six maids were fast asleep, due to the exhaustion of the working day. Peg's bed was the nearest to the door. The pair silently made their way to her bed, where Vickery placed his huge hands across her mouth, and Mrs Stark quickly tied her wrists and ankles together. Vickery gagged her, and the two of them carried her -one taking her legs the other her arms. Peggy had woken from a nightmare into a living nightmare. She tried to struggle but her bonds were too tight, also she was indeed being carried. They made their way down the twisting staircase to the reception hall at the very bottom of the three flights of steps.

Suddenly, they were outside. Peg obviously in a very frightened state wondered what her fate would be. She looked up and could see bright stars and a full moon. She heard the sound of rushing water, and was then carefully placed in the bottom of a rowing boat. Vickery and Mrs Stark got into the boat and rowed out to the centre of the river Ribble. Peggy felt what seemed like cold metal being placed around her ankle.

She heard Mrs Stark say to Vickery, "Well, your daughters' futures are now secure. Just toss her over the side." Unknown to poor Peg, they had attached a huge chain to her ankle with a large piece of metal at the other end.

"Take her gag off." shouted Mrs Stark. Vickery lifted the chain and its weight, and with great effort tossed it over the rowing boat's side.

Peg watched in horror as the chain raced after it. She knew she was about to die. She shouted, "I will haunt you for the rest of your lives!" Her body followed the weight to the bottom of the river. Her only crime in life was to be a beautiful young woman, who'd had the misfortune of meeting John Stark.

The following morning, Stark and his two sons came down for breakfast. "Where is Peggy?" he asked of

Vickery.

"Oh Sir, she decided to go back to Ireland last night Sir."

"What?" shouted Stark. "She never told me!"

Ian, the youngest lad burst into tears, James quickly followed. Vickery carried on with his lies, "Yes Sir, she just left. Such an ungrateful young woman, when you Sir provided employment for her."

Stark was indeed very saddened by Peg just leaving. He and his sons had no idea she was at the bottom of the river Ribble. Well, letters came from Ireland weeks later demanding where young peg was from a very concerned father. Stark did write back in all honesty informing them that she had just left of her own free will.

Mrs Stark started to feel some guilt, and two days later as she lay in bed she felt she could hear a voice coming from downstairs. It was a soft, female Irish voice. She got out of bed, and made her way downstairs clutching a lamp lit by a candle. As the got to the bottom of the stairs, the voice seemed to be coming from the porch. She made her way to the porch door, and slowly opened it. There was no-one there apart from a stone statue. She touched the statue, and in the light of the moon noticed the statue was a female figure. The figure although made of stone seemed to look her in the face with a frown.

"Right, I will settle you!" said Mrs Stark. She rushed upstairs to wake Vickery. She hammered on his bedroom door. "Wake up - I have a job for you!"

"What's wrong Madam?" replied a half asleep Vickery.

"Get your hammer and chisel."

With a bemused look on his face, the butler said, "Why Madam, it's the middle of the night."

Vickery got dressed and followed Mrs Stark downstairs to the front porch, where she pointed at the statue.

"Vickery, I want you to knock the head off this

statue and throw the head and statue into the river."

"But Madam, the statue has been here for years. Your husband's father purchased it some years ago."

She raised her voice. "Vickery, just do it!"

"As you wish, Ma'am." he replied.

He made his way to the stable block and came back with a hammer and chisel. He placed the chisel at the base of the statue's head and with a series of blows, the head was smashed off the rest of the statue. With the use of a wooden wheelbarrow, Vickery placed the statue and its removed head in the barrow and made the short journey down to the riverside. He raised the barrow, the statue and head made their ways to the bottom of the river.

As Vickery made his way from the river bank to the hall, he thought he heard a soft voice with an Irish accent. He also felt uncomfortable, almost as though he was being watched.

"I will haunt you for the rest of your life!"

A wind whipped up and the water rippled as he turned to make the journey back to the hall. He took one last look at the river bank behind him, and gazed at the opposite river bank. There in the dull moonlight, he could just make out a female figure on the bank. She seemed to be pointing at him. His blood froze as he recognised Peggy.

This time it was unmistakable, the figure shouted again, "I will haunt you for the rest of your life."

Vickery had one thing on his mind, total self preservation. He ran at great speed back to the hall. On entering, he saw Mrs Stark sitting at the bottom of the stairs. He shouted, "It's her, it's her!"

"What are you talking about man?" asked Mrs Stark.

"It's Peggy!" he blurted out. "She is on the river bank."

"Impossible. She is dead!" replied Mrs Stark.

With eyes the size of soup plates, Vickery told her what he had just witnessed. She then told him why the statue had to go, as she was convinced it was talking, possessed by the ghost of Peg O'Nell.

Both of them felt terrible fear.

"Madam, I cannot stay here any more. I resign my position with the family."

"Vickery, I need you, you are my right arm." she said, in an urgent manner. "If you are going, so am I!"

That night, both of them left Waddow Hall, Vickery leaving his wife and two daughters, Mrs Stark her unfaithful husband and two sons.

They made their way to Liverpool and purchased two places on a vessel, The Boundary Star, heading for St Kitts. Mrs Stark had investments in the slave trade and property on the island. But their vessel never completed the journey, and became involved in a huge Atlantic storm just off the coast of Wicklow, Ireland.

The Boundary Star capsized and both Vickery and Stark found themselves treading water in the cold, icy Atlantic. The water had an effect on both of them as they clutched each other. And in the seconds before they drowned, both turned to see what looked like a female figure standing on the water. It was indeed Peggy's ghost. She pointed at them both, and with a stony smile the ghost shouted, "I will haunt you for the rest of your life!"

Back at Waddow Hall, John stark never really missed his wife and many a young lady was invited to share his bed until he died of an alcohol related disease years later. His two sons continued to live in the hall, and years later both of them made their way into Clitheroe town and visited the Swan and Royal Hotel for a very good drink. As the alcohol flowed, they joined a card school and brought the school back to the Hall to continue the game, but also have access to more alcohol. On one game of three card brag they lost all of their money. On the second game, they lost their ancestral home. As a result of this disastrous card game, both of them were ejected from the building and a very uncertain future.

As they left the Hall for the very last time, the brothers made their way over the river at a bridge called Brungerly Park. As they crossed the bridge they looked down the river, and noticed a female figure on the banking wearing what looked to be a nightdress. The figure seemed to glide, not walk - but glide towards them.

"It's Peggy!" shouted James, looking his brother in the face. The ghostly figure seemed to make a gesture with her hand to follow her. They scrambled down from the bridge and down to the river bank. They could not see her.

Then James shouted, "There she is, on the water!"

Both Men watched in amazement as Peggy stood on the water's surface in the centre of the river. Then she pointed to the river bank in front of them, gesturing them to look for something. Slowly, very slowly, Peggy descended beneath the water. Both boys were shocked by what they had just witnessed. They made their way to the area that she had pointed to.

"Hey, there is some writing in the mud!"

In clear handwriting on the mud, read the words "Peg O' Nell" and, "I shall take a life every seven years, or a cockerel every New Year's Day."

In the 1930's the Girl Guides association purchased the hall. It was indeed ideal for camping in the huge grounds, and the hall's many rooms ideal for accommodation and indeed conferences.

Every New Year's Day, the staff place a cockerel in a cage in Peg's old room, as a way of appeasing her spirit and indeed her wishes. In the 20th century the cockerel was found dead on fourteen occasions and in 2006 also. Peggy's ghost still haunts the river bank opposite the hall where she was murdered all those years ago.

In October 1987 two lads were carrying out their trade, salmon poaching. These boys had the best trainers and Levi's in Clitheroe and their parents could not understand why they had so much money. They were told, "It's the paper round." They were in fact supplying the local hotels and fishmongers with top quality salmon.

One bright October evening in 1987, the lads made their way down to the river, the bright moonlight illuminated the area. They threw the net across the width of the river and started to walk up stream. One lad was in the grounds of Waddow Hall, while his mate was on the Clitheroe banking.

Suddenly, they heard a noise almost like a young girl singing. Peggy's ghost appeared out of the river mist. The lad on the Clitheroe banking wasn't very brave - he dropped the net and scampered back home, leaving his mate on the Waddow side. On seeing the ghost, he dived into the cold, icy waters of the river, and fully dressed - he swam across. Half way across, he felt something grab at his ankle. He screamed in terror, but with brute strength, he fought his way across to the other side of the river. He realised that the salmon net had twisted itself all around his left leg. He got to the opposite bank in exhaustion, and for a few seconds he lay on his back in the mud on the river bank gasping for air. His heart hammered in his chest, he glanced to his left and there it was. Peggy's ghost was just a few feet away. He noticed that she had a long white gown on, with puffed up sleeves. The ghostly figure turned to look at him, his hair stood on end as he noticed that where there should have been a face was indeed a deep black cavity. He got to his feet and ran back to Clitheroe at great speed. He never, ever visited the river again.

In 2006 a district midwife nurse drove her mini metro from a western Ribble valley village in the early hours of the morning. She made her way down to Brungerly Bridge opposite Waddow Hall. As her car was about to cross the bridge, she saw a figure standing in the centre of the bridge. She wound her window down and shouted out of the window towards the figure.

"Excuse me, I would like to cross the bridge please."

There was no answer. The nurse noticed that her

car headlights were shining straight through the apparition. The district nurse panicked and selected first, second, and third gears and drove straight towards the ghostly apparition. Suddenly the ghostly object entered the engine, then the dash board and straight out of the back of the car. She drove at great speed home, horrified by what she had just experienced. On getting home she woke her father up, and told him what had happened to her.

In a very annoyed voice he shouted back, "No, you have not seen a ghost - you have run someone over!"

Her father telephoned the police, and a constable was dispatched down to the bridge. He found no evidence of any road traffic accident at the bridge and then contacted every hospital in the area. There had been no admissions that night. It was put down to the ghost of Peg O'Nell, whose only crime in life was to be a beautiful young woman who had the misfortune of meeting John Stark that fateful morning in the City of Liverpool.

Local folk-law tells us that Peggy will take the life of someone in the river by drowning them every seven years. And sadly over the years many people have drowned in sight of Waddow Hall. Certainly, that stretch of river can be very atmospheric, especially in the autumn when the mists blow in from the sea and blanket the bridge and indeed the river bank itself. You just never know when Peg will next appear.

Chapter 12
Ghostly Tales from the Road

One warm June evening, Mr John Burrows of Preston, Lancashire drove to Kendal to see his mother. He came off the M6 at Crooklands and thought he would take the scenic route into Kendal via Milnthorpe. He made his way towards the hamlet of Hincaster, and as he drove round a bend, he saw a female figure standing by the side of the road. She looked very distressed, and raised her hand for John to stop his vehicle. He pulled over, and immediately became aware that she was injured. The side of her dress was torn and soaked in blood. John jumped out of the vehicle, opened the passenger door and gently coaxed her into the front seat. He slammed the door shut, raced around the car and got back into the driving seat.

"What's happened love?" he enquired.

The young women was in a highly distressed state,

"Please take me to the hospital! Please!" she screamed.

"Okay" said John in a reassuring voice.

He put his foot down, driving quickly through the villages of Hincaster, Sedgwick and Natland. He tried to get a conversation going with his passenger. She said that she had been hit by a car near Hincaster and that the driver had not stopped. John glanced down at her side, she was losing blood. He had to get her to hospital at great speed, or she could die. He asked her name and she told him that she was called Candice.

As the frantic journey continued, she fell in and out of consciousness. Soon they were in the village of Natland, and Kendal was in sight. John was aware of the Westmorland County Hospital in the town centre, up near the golf club. His car raced up to the road to the hospital. The traffic lights were on red, but as it was an emergency, he chanced it and went straight through the red lights. John heard a car horn blasting away at him and he very nearly collided with a police car.

Suddenly the hospital was in sight and he made his way into the car park outside the casualty building. Just as he was reversing to park the car, to his amazement his passenger Candice opened the car door and rushed away, limping at great speed into the casualty department.

John parked the car and locked it up and was about to follow Candice into the hospital when he heard a voice shout. "Oye! Did you drive through those red lights?"

John turned round and saw two police officers.

"Yes, I did officer. I'm sorry, but I had this women in my car - she was badly injured. She is in the casualty right now."

One of the officers made his way in to the building and two minutes later came back out again.

"Right Sir. There is no-one apart from staff in the building." said the officer.

John had a bemused look on his face."I swear to you, I brought this young woman to the hospital she was badly injured, Just look at my car seat, it's absolutely soaked in blood. The two officers advanced to John's car and looked at the seats. There was no evidence of any blood on any of the seats.

On being shown this, John was horrified. "I swear I picked her up."

The officers informed John that he was going to be breathalysed and reported for dangerous driving. A breathalyser was promptly produced.

"Right Sir. We want you to give us a breath sample."

"Officer, I am not drunk, I brought this young woman to the hospital. She was seriously injured .I swear I am not lying!"

The police officer said, "Sir, your driving is abysmal. Do you realise that you could have killed not only yourself but both of us as well?"

Suddenly a doctor came out of the casualty building

and noticed that John Burrows looked very agitated.

"What's the problem gentlemen?" asked the doctor.

"Well, this gentleman has just committed a very serious driving offence. But his breath is clear of alcohol."

He looked at the breathalyser kit.

"Doctor!" shouted Burrows, "I swear I brought a young woman in her twenties to this hospital some 10 minutes ago. She was wearing a blue dress with a white cardigan, she had serious injuries and informed me that she had been hit by a car near Hincaster."

The doctor looked Burrows in the eye, "Blue dress you say, and white cardigan?"

"Yes doctor, although her cardigan and the left side of her torso were saturated in blood."

"Officers, would you mind if I took this gentleman in to my office for a moment?" asked the doctor of the two confused looking police officers.

"You can doctor, but we are going to take him to the police station for a urine test."

"I can do that here," said the doctor.

Burrows followed the doctor to his office at the back of the Accident and Emergency department. He was offered a cigarette and gratefully accepted one.

John introduced himself, the doctor had a look of deep concern on his face, "Mr Burrows, I have been a casualty doctor here for the past four years. Some fifteen months ago I heard about a road traffic victim being brought in from the Hincaster area. She was called Candice Blundell, she was just twenty three years old. On arriving she had lost a huge amount of blood, and had some terrible injuries to her stomach and liver. She was wearing a blue dress and a white cardigan saturated in blood. I got three lines in to her, but her blood loss was too great. No sooner had we tried to restore her levels, she lost blood at the same rate. The surgeons tried desperately to stop the bleeding, but could not. She died in theatre four hours from arriving here at the Westmorland County. By some strange coincidence, Mr Burrows it was indeed this very evening 15 months ago that she was admitted to this department. Your story is quite remarkable, Mr Burrows. I must ask you something." The doctor looked at John with a serious look on his face, "Please, you're not one of these people that gets a kick out of other people's misery are you? Her death upset all of us that tried so desperately to save her."

Burrows was furious at the doctors question. "I do not live in the area," he shouted. "And I get no pleasure from this whatsoever, I swear to you on my life I picked a young woman up this evening on the road verge just before the hamlet of Hincaster."

"Okay," sighed the Doctor, "I still have a press report about this tragedy in my locker."

The doctor left Burrows and went to look in his locker. John thought to himself, "Am I going mad? It's very likely I will lose my driving license, as a result of the traffic lights and the police vehicle."

The doctor re-entered the room.

"Here we are," he said, passing John a Westmorland Gazette from May 1997.

"Second column down," he said, "There's a picture of her too."

John looked in amazement, twenty three year old Candice Blundell from Hincaster died as a result of a road traffic accident. The picture confirmed that this was the young woman he had brought to casualty. John continued to read the report. A local farmer had been arrested for hitting her with a baling spike, and not stopping after committing the accident. This extraordinary visit to the hospital would stay with John Burrows, and the doctor for a very long time.

For our next tale from the road, we are going to make our way to the beautiful North Yorkshire Market town of Skipton. Tony Wiseman and Kenneth Dwyer were very good mates, both lads had attended the same primary and secondary schools. And like most young men they had a keen interest in football, the pub and young ladies. On leaving school they both applied for the fire service, and both were accepted. They trained together and were both employed in the town as full time firemen.

Now obviously, being a fire fighter is a very dangerous job, and both men had promised each other in the event of either of them losing their lives, the other would make sure that their children were looked after. Both lads had been best man at one another's wedding, and indeed shared the same holidays with wives and children. These two were literally best-mates.

Ken had two children, a daughter of nine and a son, Robert aged six. Ken sadly was going to lose his life, but not due to his employment as a fire fighter. Ken had a powerful Kawasaki motorbike, and there was nothing he enjoyed more than going for 'a burn' as he called it.

One warm Sunday morning in 2009, Ken kissed his wife Jenny, and told her that he was just going for a spin, and that he'd be back at dinner time. He climbed onto the Kawasaki, and made his way onto the A59 towards the city of Leeds. The weather conditions were perfect. He made his way towards a place called Blubberhouses near Harrogate. He noticed the stretch of road in front of him was completely free of traffic.

"Right, let's see what this baby can do!" he said, his wrist squeezing the accelerator as he kicked down on the gears and felt pure power from the bike's engine, his speed increasing with every second.

Poor Ken had no idea that around the next bend, a wagon carrying scaffolding poles had lost four poles off the back of the vehicle. They were lain across the road surface. Ken came around the corner at seventy five miles an hour. He hit a scaffolding pole, and his bike was lifted by the impact and he was thrown clean off the bike. On making contact with the ground, his neck was broken on impact.

A few hours later, Ken's best mate Tony had a phone call from Jenny who sobbed into the telephone, "It's Ken, he's dead!" she sobbed.

Tony looked at the ceiling for a second or two, "What? How?" he shouted down the phone.

"Killed on that stupid bike of his!" she screamed down the phone, with tears streaming down her face. Tony instantly remembered his promise to Ken to make sure his kids were alright. Tony rushed out of his house and got into his car, and drove to Ken's house. On arriving, he noticed a police vehicle outside the home and on entering he saw a WPC comforting Jenny and the daughter.

Tony whispered to Jenny, "Where is Robert?"

"Upstairs." said Jenny, in a deeply distressed voice.

"Does he know yet?" whispered Tony.

"No." Jenny sobbed. "Could you please tell him?"

"Yes, of course I will." said Tony. He made his way upstairs and noticed six year old Robert on his play station, happily sitting on his bed humming to himself.

Tony sat down on the bed next to him. "Robert, I am so sorry I have some very sad news to tell you." Tony thought of the most diplomatic way he could tell the six year old that his father was dead. He put his arm around the boy. Tony took a deep breath. "Robert, your daddy has been involved in a terrible accident, I am so sorry, he has passed away," said Tony, in the most caring voice he could muster.

To Tony's huge shock and surprise, little Robert turned round and looked him in the eye with a confident smile on his face.

"It's okay Uncle Tony, my dad has just been here a few minutes ago and told me all about it. He says I have to be brave and look after mum."

Our next tale from the road comes from a very dangerous hair-pin bend aptly named the "Devils Elbow."

This is a section of road near a village called Read in the Ribble Valley.

Keith Mason of nearby town Great Harwood worked for the Prestige cooker factory in Burnley. At Christmas 1968 they were extremely busy and there was plenty of overtime for all employees. Keith clocked off at 8.00pm on Christmas Eve, got into his Humber Sceptre and began his journey from Burnley to Great Harwood. The weather conditions that night were not good, high winds and sleet in the air, and as he advanced toward Read village he noticed that he was the only driver on the road. His windscreen wipers were working at the maximum speed to keep the screen clear.

Suddenly, he was about to enter the accident hotspot known as the Devils Elbow. Over the years there had been many accidents on the "elbow," mainly due to drivers who had never been on this tricky section of road before. Keith slowed down to a crawl as he started to drive round the elbow, his car headlamps picked out a motorcycle on its side by the pavement, and a person dressed in motorbike leathers. He was standing next to his bike, holding what looked like a plastic petrol container. He signalled to Keith to stop, Keith mirrored, signalled and manoeuvred to the side of the pavement next to the bike's rider.

He wound the window down and shouted, "Are you okay, mate?"

The motorcyclist had a helmet with a visor and just nodded, Keith noticed he was holding the fuel container.

"Do you want a lift mate? I can take you to the garage to buy some petrol." Again the rider just nodded,

"Okay lad, get in the car. I will take you in to Whalley, to the petrol station."

Keith opened the passenger door and the motorcyclist got in and Keith signalled to drive off. He could smell the strong aroma of petrol but also alcohol. Keith kept his eyes on the road as the conditions outside became very dangerous, heavy snow was falling and he was determined to get home. But this was Christmas Eve, goodwill to all men. He asked his passenger where he had come from. To Keith's amazement the rider had not taken his helmet off, or even lifted the visor which was completely covering his face. Keith's first impression was this guy is ignorant, "I have gone out of my way to help him, and he can't even be bothered to talk to me." He thought.

Soon, Whalley was in sight. "Right mate, there's the petrol station," he said to his passenger.

All of a sudden, the hair on Keith's head stood up, as he glanced to his left and was looking at a completely empty passenger seat. The motorcyclist had literally vanished into thin air, even the petrol container had gone. Keith turned the car around and made his way back to Great Harwood at some speed, shaking with fright.

On getting home he had a stiff drink and told his family about this unusual ghostly encounter. His work mates also found his story very humorous.

Years later, in the Wellington pub in Great Harwood, Keith ordered a drink from the bar and noticed a young lad was standing nearby. The lad had a confused look on his face.

"Are you okay mate?" asked Keith.

"No, not really," he replied, "No one believes me."

"Believes what?" said Keith.

"Well last night I was driving from Burnley to here, the weather was appalling - lots of sleet and snow. Well, I entered the Devils Elbow, and there was this lad standing by the pavement with a petrol can in his hand. Keith eyes lit up, as he realised that his own story had been confirmed.

Chapter 13
Heroic Ghosts

In the Market town of Clitheroe is a rather picturesque street known as Church Brow. At the top of the brow is St Mary's Parish Church and the Parish Church office. All along the steep street, there is a collection of rather beautiful Georgian houses.

Let's turn the clock back to the year 1907. John and Edith Mercer had just got married for the first time at the age of 47. They purchased number 11 Church Brow. The last thing they had planned was to become parents, but Edith conceived and gave birth to a very healthy baby boy. They called him Peter and looked on this little boy as a gift from the good Lord.

Sadly, just before his fifth birthday, Peter contracted scarlet fever and died in his bedroom surrounded by his loved ones. His parents had their hearts broken in two. Losing their beloved son was a very painful experience and the Mercer's never really got over the pain of losing Peter at such a tender age.

We now pick up the story some 25 years later. Window cleaner Mr John Gorham cleaned the windows of number 11 Church Brow. It was a lovely, warm August afternoon with blue skies and light, gentle winds. As was always the case, John Gorham would wet the window pane then clean the window with his chamois leather and rub it dry with another cloth.

Window cleaners have to be very diplomatic, when cleaning windows; you will come across the kinds of things that George Formby would sing about. Gorham suddenly noticed on the other side of the window pain a little boy dressed in a sailor suit with golden hair and a huge smile on his face. The little lad waved at him, John would smile and wave back, and the little boy would run into all three top bedrooms to watch Gorham clean the windows. John always enjoyed seeing the little boy, and looked forward to visiting the house.

After some fourteen months, John thought to himself, that little boy is not getting any bigger and he is always wearing the same clothes. In all the times Gorham had seen him, the boy had never made a noise or attempted to speak, he just smiled and waved at Gorham.

He knocked on the next door to get his payment, a house owned by Mrs Harrison. John told her what he had seen. "Oh, Mr Gorham," said Mrs Harrison, "You are seeing things. The Mercer's did have a little boy but he died a quarter of a century ago."

He then went next door and knocked on Mrs Mercer's front door. She opened the door, Gorham's words were, "Mrs Mercer, I have no intention of upsetting you and please forgive me if I do so, but I feel it is my duty to inform you that every time I clean the windows upstairs there is always a little boy who waves and smiles at me."

A huge smile spread across Mrs Mercer's face. "Oh, Mr Gorham, don't worry. It's my little boy Peter, He is still with me."

Not too far from Church Brow is St Mary's Church Yard and as you enter the church yard on the far right near the railings is a grave with a very touching story from a very loving and affectionate wife called Helen Southworth. Her husband William was indeed a true hero and gentleman.

In the winter of 2010 a group of friends got permission to spend a night in the 1738 grade 2 listed public house, The Lower Buck in Waddington. Today, this famous village is part of the Ribble Valley – but traditionally, Waddington belongs to the West Riding of Yorkshire. The group visiting the Lower Buck had heard about ghostly goings on and wanted to spend a night on the flagstone floor in the bar area.

The main purpose of the visit was to raise money for the Air Ambulance charity, and they thought that spending a ghostly night in this ancient building would be great fun and a spooky challenge. None of them had any idea that during their visit they would have a very paranormal experience.

One of the group, Jenny - took a photograph of a tall figure near the door and what looked like a little girl next to him. The photograph was so clear that it got printed on the front page of the Clitheroe Advertiser Newspaper. Many fans of the Lower Buck believe the ghostly character in Jenny's photograph to be, Landlord William Southworth, who loved that building so much he could not bare to leave it.

On a beautiful May day in 1833, William Southworth made his way to the local butchers in Waddington. On entering the building, he was shocked and saddened to see the butcher Thomas Chatburn beating his wife up. William could not just stand and watch this, and he intervened by rescuing Mrs Chatburn. He took her outside and sat her on the wall comforting her.

William had no idea, but that night in an alcohol fuelled temper - Chatburn came bursting in to the Lower Buck Inn, shouting, "I understand that you have been telling persons that I have been assaulting my wife?"

"No!" demanded William, "all I did was intervene, I just wanted to help her."

Chatburn's face contorted. "I will have you!" he shouted, in a drunken state. Suddenly he lurched forward to attack Southworth, and it looked for a moment like William Southworth intended to teach Chatburn a lesson. To his horror, Chatburn suddenly produced a Butcher's knife and sank its metal blade four times in to William's heart. Mortally wounded, he staggered outside and knelt on the cobble-stones in front of the Inn, with his wife screaming by his side in anguish, William passed away. His wife insisted his courageous story should be put on his grave tablet and today you can read the whole story.

The 1758 Sun Inn is a hugely popular hostelry situated in the award winning village of Chipping, If the walls could talk, they would tell us some quite amazing stories from the pages of time. One such story begins in the autumn of 1835. A young woman of 20 years arrived in the village called Elizabeth Dean. She was a pretty young lady, and was quickly offered a job as a Scullery Maid in the Inn. She worked with a fellow Maid called Elsie Trainer. They enjoyed each other's company and became very close friends. One day a handsome young lad entered the Inn called James Freeman.

He took one look at Lizzy and his heart skipped a beat. It was love at first sight, and after a short period of courting, he proposed to her. She immediately accepted, and the pair made their way across the cobbled street to the Church Saint Bartholomew's, situated adjacent to the Sun Inn. There they had a meeting with the Vicar and arranged a date to get married.

Lizzy was so happy, a handsome husband to be, and a nice cottage to live in - all her dreams had come true. Two days before the wedding was due to take place, James got cold feet and told Lizzy, "I am so sorry I don't want to marry you. I am in love with your friend Elsie." Lizzy's heart was snapped in two.

"How could this be?" she cried. The relationship became very tense, as she continued to work in the Inn with Elsie, who in the meantime – had accepted a marriage proposal from Lizzy's lost love, James Freeman.

On the day of Elsie and James' wedding, Lizzy Dean made her way upstairs to the Inn's attic. She opened the window that overlooked the church entrance. With tears streaming down her face, she removed the window curtain cord, and made a noose. She then tied the end of the cord to the metal bedstead. She gazed out of the window. Suddenly a carriage arrived with Freeman and his best man. She watched as they made their way up the main path to the church. A short while later the bride and her father arrived, who also made their way in to St Bartholomew's.

From her vantage point, Lizzy could hear the sound of the wedding march. The pain in her chest was crippling. "How could this happen?" she muttered to herself.

Suddenly she heard the sound of the church bells ring out joyously. But Lizzy felt nothing other than deep emotional pain, she had been jilted by her fiancée and by her best friend. She quickly wrote a note, and gripped it tightly in her right fist. With tears running down her face, she climbed out of the window - her slight frame just allowing this. Lizzy placed the noose around her neck and, with her feet dangling out of the window, she waited for the time to jump. She did not have to wait very long. The church door opened and out came James and Elsie, with huge smiles on their faces. They were followed by family and friends who were also joyful, delighted to be a part of the happy occasion.

Suddenly somebody screamed and everybody's attention was taken by the figure hanging out of the attic window by the neck. The atmosphere went from jubilation to horror in a matter of seconds. Lizzy was indeed hanging by her neck some 30 feet above the ground from the attic window.

Villagers including James and Elsie rushed from the scene, the reception that was planned to take place at the Inn was cancelled. Poor Lizzy's body was cut down. It was noticed that in her right hand there was a tightly clenched, short letter. The sad note said simply; "I wish to be buried at the entrance to St Bartholomew's, so James and Elsie will have to walk past my grave every time they go to church."

Well, to this day she is indeed buried at the entrance to the church, but our story is only beginning. James and Elsie both felt the pressure of living in the village and so close to Lizzy's gravestone. The tragic death of the young woman had a huge effect on them, as Lizzy had probably intended.

They decided to start again elsewhere and moved

away to the City of Carlisle. Lizzy lost her life in very sad circumstances and her ghost has been featured on a variety of TV and radio programmes over the years.

I received a telephone call from a Scottish chap one night in 1999. He was on holiday with his wife and two daughters, staying in Lytham St Annes. They had a drive out into the village of Chipping, where the mother and her two daughters made their way to the local furniture factory show-house.

The father, Neil Sherringham, went into the Sun Inn for a pint, it was just after 11.30 am. As he entered, he was surprised to find the Inn empty, apart from the landlord Steve. He ordered a pint of bitter and sat by himself in the Snug area of the bar. Neil took his pipe out and lit it, and as he did so, he suddenly became aware of someone else in the room. There in the corner standing near the Snug door he could see a young girl with ringlets in her hair, wearing clothing from a different period. Her dress looked like it had been washed thousands of times, in fact she gave an almost pantomime appearance. He tried to make vocal contact with her but she gazed in to the room with a look of deep sadness on her face as if he was not there.

"Good morning," he said. There was no answer. And then to his great surprise the female figure walked into the centre of the room, walking through two tables and out through the old, bricked up door from the 1800s. Nearly choking on his pipe he rushed into the other bar shouting for the landlord.

Steve came down the stairs. "What's wrong mate?" he asked.

"I have just seen this girl walk through the wall," said Neil, clearly in shock.

Steve the landlord just laughed. "Don't worry mate you have just seen the ghost of Elizabeth Dean, she has been with us since the 5th of November 1835!"

The Sun Inn is a regular on Paranormal TV and

radio programmes. I have never seen her myself, but I am sure you will agree, she was a very brave young lady. Today at the Inn they have a restaurant called Lizzies Lounge, and if you wish, you can also visit her grave, as many tourists do each year, situated just as she requested, by the entrance to St Bartholomew's Church.

Chapter 14
Dukes Brow, Blackburn

In the year 1642 the English civil war started. The King had many supporters, one being Gilbert De Houghton of Houghton Towers near Preston. He wrote to King Charles, "Sir, I shall take Blackburn, Burnley and Clitheroe before the new year, I promise you sir the Royal Standard will be flying above all three towns before the new year starts."

Now Gilbert was an exceptionally wealthy man but not the best of military commanders. He armed and clothed a huge army from the Fylde Coast and they set off to attack and capture the town of Blackburn on the Christmas Eve of 1642. He had some considerable fire power in the form of canon and infantry. His battalion arrived at a place called Dukes Brow, over looking the East Lancashire town. He ordered his artillery to open fire on Blackburn from their vantage point on Dukes Brow.

In the town, two Colonels, Starkie and Shuttleworth had anticipated the attack and had trenches built around the town. They intended to hold for parliament, but cannon fire rained down on the town from Dukes Brow. The Colonels informed their men that an infantry attack was imminent. The defenders kept their heads beneath the trench parapet as the cannon balls were being fired indiscriminately and causing quite a lot of damage. Then suddenly the barrage stopped.

"Right men, prepare for the infantry assault!" shouted Colonel Shuttleworth.

But nothing happened, because on Dukes Brow a huge argument was taking place with Gilbert De Houghton and his men. His Battalion Commander said, "Sir, we do not mind dying for the King Sir, or indeed your good self, but this is Christmas Eve, we should all be at home with our families."

Houghton was furious, "Attack Blackburn, now I

order you all to attack. I have paid for your uniforms and your weapons. Attack blast you!"

His men refused and about-turned to march back to the Fylde and their families. Houghton went red with rage. He knew that he could not arrest every man.

In the meantime, in the trenches in Blackburn Starkie and Shuttleworth shouted, "Lads, they're retreating - up and after them!"

The Blackburn defenders got to the top of Dukes Brow, just as the rear guard was leaving, and an exchange of fire took place. This action took the lives of quite a few men on both sides, with many rounds of ammunition fired by both sides. Shuttleworth was delighted he captured all of Houghton's canons and a huge amount of powder and muskets. These were taken to Whalley for safe keeping. Houghton's dream of taking all three towns had been a complete failure. Had he chosen another month, he may just have pulled it off.

We are now going to turn the clock forward to a warm summer's day in 1995, Mrs Joan Davidson ran a busy Bed and Breakfast business on Dukes Brow. She owned a huge Victorian house, her five children had all left home and she was left with this enormous house. Well, the idea of the Bed and Breakfast took off and she was kept busy all year round.

The weather was very pleasant and she decided to have a look at her vegetable patch, an area she had not taken much of an interest for the past few years. She got a fork from the garden shed and decided to dig the patch over. Mrs Davidson began to turn the soil over. It was hard, but pleasant work. Half way through the patch she heard a metallic sound and looked at the soil.

"Looks like a cannon ball!" she said and another twist of the fork revealed what looked like a broken spur. At the end of the dig she had unearthed two cannon balls, some flat musket balls and the spur. She placed them in a seed try and took them inside and placed them on the side of the sink.

Suddenly the telephone rang. She washed her hands and quickly dried them, rushing in to the living room. She picked up the phone, "Blackburn 343421," she said. On the other end of the phone was an Australian person.

"Have you rooms please for my wife and I and my two daughters? We want to visit Blackburn to visit my Grandfather's ancestral home."

"Yes, I do have rooms for you all," said Mrs Davidson.

"Oh thanks," said the Australian voice, "We will be with you tomorrow afternoon." The Australian family arrived the following day. They parked in front of the B&B and knocked on the front door.

Mrs Davidson opened the door with a warm smile,

"Please come this way, if you would like to go to the front room I will make a cup of tea for you, and then I will show you to your rooms." Joan made her way to the kitchen. She put the kettle on and placed the tea bags in the pot. Suddenly she heard hysterical screaming and shouting coming from her living room where the Australians were sitting. As she made her way from the kitchen she was met by the family running down the corridor pushing her out of the way. The Australians rushed outside and got in their car, all physically shaken and obviously very distressed. They drove off at great speed, the wheels of their vehicle leaving blue smoke in the air as they departed. Joan took a deep inhale of breath, and made her way through to the living room.

"Has my cat made a mess in there?" she said, "What could have possibly happened to scare the Australian family away?" She entered the living room, and was shocked by the scene that lay before her. The settee was on its side, a picture hung awkwardly from the wall, and a lampshade was on the floor. Joan was very upset, and couldn't understand what had happened. She was delighted the next day, when the telephone rang. On the other end she heard the Australian voice,

"So sorry dear for leaving your house in such a hurry!" said the customer.

"I should think so." said Joan, "Why did you leave without saying a word?"

"Well," said the Australian, "we were sat in your front room, and all of a sudden these three soldiers walked straight out of the wall, and through my wife and daughters."

"Soldiers?" said Joan, completely and utterly amazed at what she was hearing.

"Yes, soldiers!" repeated the Australian, "They had leather jerkins on and bandoliers across their chests, goatee beards, and feathers in their caps. They walked straight through my wife and kids, they are still traumatized now," he said.

Joan sighed. "Well, thank you for telling me."

Well, in Blackburn you cannot keep things secret, and it was only a matter of time before the town heard about the ghostly royalist soldiers. And her story got in the local newspaper, quickly followed by the national press.

It was after the publication of the national newspaper that Joan was contacted by two professors from York University, who visited her Dukes Brow home. She told them about that day and also how she had found the cannon balls and the spur in her vegetable garden.

The professors' eyes lit up with excitement, "Mrs Davidson, can we please have a look at the items you dug up?"

"Of course you may," she said and brought the items to the living room where both gentlemen were seated. The cannon balls were of great interest to both men, as indeed all the items.

"Right, Mrs Davidson, our theory is as follows. We both conduct experiments relating to paranormal activities at York University. We believe that what has happened in your case is Martindale syndrome."

"Please enlighten me gentlemen," said Mrs Davidson, who had no idea what the men were talking about.

"Well in 1952 in the city of York, a plumbers mate called Harry Martindale was working in a cellar at the mansion house behind York Minster, when he heard the sound of a very loud trumpet. Then suddenly out of the cellar wall came a white horse with a roman soldier riding it. Then, the horse and its rider were followed by a platoon of Roman infantry. None of them made eye contact with Martindale, some even went straight through him. Martindale was glued to the spot in pure terror. As he took in the situation surrounding him, he noticed he could only see the soldiers from their knees, their feet were indeed missing. Suddenly the sound of the trumpet faded away and Martindale was left in silence. He shook his head, and asked himself how do I explain that? He told his boss, who just laughed at him.

His story reached the Evening press and Harry was the butt of many a city joke. Some two weeks later however, no one laughed at him, as there was still more work to do in the cellar. In the exact area that Harry had been working in, soil had been removed from the cellar floor, and a Roman road discovered, giving evidence that this was indeed the gateway to the huge barracks and the Roman city of Eborachum."

The professors then informed Mrs Davidson, "You were the first person to touch the cannon balls and indeed other items since 1642. We believe that like Martindale, you opened a gateway in to a different time and brought it to life. Mrs Davidson was indeed shocked and her answer was, "Perhaps that's what ghosts are."

Chapter 15
The Townley Hall Chapel

We always associate the Jackobite rebellion with the Scottish highlanders, but there was indeed an English regiment of foot who fought with the Young Pretenders army in 1745. They were led by an exceptionally brave officer by the name of Colonel Francis Townley of Townley Hall, Burnley.

Bonnie Prince Charlie landed on Ericksay in the Outer Hebrides. He was on a mission to put a Stuart on the throne of England and restore the Catholic faith across the land. The Highlanders gathered and invaded England, pushing any opposition away. This invading army marched down Shap Fell and into the Lake District town of Kendal. There waiting for them was the Mayor of Kendal, Mr John Firth. He was an excellent negotiator.

"Take all our food, all of our alcohol, but please - leave our women alone," he pleaded. The Prince and the Clansmen respected this and advanced through Kendal without causing the residents any harm. It was indeed in Kendal that the Prince proclaimed himself King of England.

The invasion crept south and in the city of Lancaster, the Clansmen were joined by Colonel Townley and his Manchester regiment, all of whom were Englishmen. Colonel Townley could speak fluent French and had no difficulty in conversing with the Young Pretender, he felt very proud to serve under him. They advanced to the city of Derby, for a conference.

In the meantime in the city of London there was total panic. The banks were being besieged by people horrified about losing their savings to the Scottish hoards. And on the other side of the channel, the French army were just waiting to invade. All the French needed was the signal to set off across the channel.

In the city of Derby there was a heated exchange of words amongst the Highlanders officers, and a huge decision was made to retreat back to Scotland. No one really knows why this decision was made. It could be overstretched supply lines or perhaps a fear of what lay ahead of them. Certainly the Duke of Cumberland and General Wade had organised their battalions to put up resistance and indeed push them back north.

The Prince sadly said, "Gentlemen, we shall regroup in the highlands and attack the English in areas not known to them." This huge army set off, heading back home, following the same route that they had made their invasion a short time ago.

On reaching Kendal this time around, the Scots were cold, hungry and in no mood to negotiate with the town's Mayor. The main route to Scotland was indeed through the town centre and an area known as Finkle Street. The Kendal residents were quite aware that this time the Scots would be extremely aggressive and in a rape and pillage mood. The Mayor, Mr Firth, gave orders that all females must leave the town and shelter on the local fells. A barricade was quickly assembled at the top of Finkle Street, and local men took up firing positions.

Standing behind the barricade were three local lads whose selfless bravery would go down in the town's history, in a similar fashion to the famous Alamo story on the Mexican border.

Local men Summerville, Hayton and Storey, took stock of their situation, and as the first highlanders made their way in to the top of Finkle Street, Hayton shouted, "Fire!"

The Kendal defenders volley fired, killing some 24 Highlanders instantly. They watched in horror as many more advanced to their positions.

Hayton managed to re-load just in time to kill another Scot at point-blank-range. The flood of Highlanders entering the street was indeed too strong for these brave Kendal boys to hold. The Scots showed no mercy, but not before Summerville, Hayton and Storey had fixed bayonets. All three died in the defence of the Auld Grey town.

But in the town centre a legend was being formed. The Carradus family consisted of Michael, his wife Edith and their three daughters. Michael insisted that his wife and daughters take shelter on the fells with the other women. His youngest daughter Catherine was five years old and had almost knee length hair of pure gold, almost straw coloured. Somehow in the panic to leave the town, she had become confused and had been left alone in the house. Outside hordes of hungry, dishevelled and footsore Highlanders made their way through the town, with the Duke of Cumberland's red coats hot on their tail.

Five year old Catherine went down stairs to the front door, and as she opened it, and looked outside, her appearance had an immediate effect on the Highlanders. Various groups of them gave her a wide berth, some were actually very scared of her. She stood there in her long white night gown, and as the wind caught her hair, she gave an angelic impression. Some of the Scots knelt in prayer,

"Oh Lord God has sent us an angel," some cried out. Catherine's presence had a huge effect on the town's safety, and apart from the Finkle Street actions at the barricades - the town was left relatively unscathed by this huge retreating Army.

To this day the legend of the "Angel of Kendal" is well known, and for many years the town had a public house called the Angel, on the very sight of the old Carradus family home.

As the last Highlander left the town, elements of the Duke of Cumberland's Red Coats entered the town. The Duke actually taking refreshments in the same building that the Young Pretender had also done so only a matter of hours before. He visited the barricades on Finkle Street and praised Hayton and his men who had given their lives to defend the town.

The Young Pretender and his bedraggled army

reached the City of Carlisle and its historic Castle.

It's here where our story starts. Colonel Townley and his Manchester regiment were ordered by the Prince to hold Carlisle and in effect act as rearguard for him and the Highlanders to escape back to safety and in his case to France.

The Colonel addressed his men, "Gentlemen, we have been ordered to hold Carlisle at all costs." His men took to the ramparts and their defensive positions. The same day they were attacked by the Dukes Red Coats that outnumbered them some 5 to 1, but the Manchesters put up stiff resistance, even though the journey from Derby had exhausted them. They held for three days, giving Bonny Prince Charlie time to escape English justice.

Colonel Francis Townley, totally outnumbered, surrendered Carlisle, they had no ammunition left and little food, and had distinguished themselves. On being captured the Colonel demanded to be treated as a prisoner of war, informing his captors that he had served in the past as an officer with the French Army. Although this was indeed true, he was told that if anything, this statement would go against him. He was informed by the Duke and indeed General Wade that he was no prisoner of war, but a common traitor. The Colonel and what was left of his command were taken down to the city of London, and thrown into Newgate Prison to await trial. Colonel Townley was paraded in front of a court held in the City in 1746, and along with his fellow officers ordered to be executed by hang, drawing and quartering, a particularly painful death.

The Colonel watched the execution of his fellow officers and bravely climbed up on to the execution rostrum. Watched by a huge crowd, he turned for a short while almost looking in the direction of Burnley and his beloved Townley Hall. In seconds he was subjected to the sort of pain we can only imagine. His head was placed on a pike and put on display at Temple Bar in London for all to gloat over. His beloved wife Mary made the long journey from Burnley to remove her husband's head and bring it back to the ancestral home.

There the Colonel's head was placed in a wicker basket with a napkin over it, and on rare occasions inspected by family members. Years later, the Colonel's head was placed inside the Chapel at the Hall, behind one of the many oak panels.

And there it remained until the 1940s when an inquisitive person had mistakenly opened the oak panel. This person recorded that the skull had some mattered hair still on it, and a large hole where the pike had gone through it in 1746.

It was then decided that the head be interned at St Peters Church, Burnley, and to this day the head remains there.

Townley Hall is a truly excellent building and every room does indeed have a story to tell. Colonel Francis Townley was an excellent musician, and could play the organ and the spinet beautifully. It is said that on the retreat from Derby, he stopped at Lancaster's Priory Church, and played the organ there. Years later the same organ found its way to Whalley Parish Church.

Townley Hall is owned and run by Burnley council and also serves as a very popular art gallery. The building is closed every night, and burglar alarms turned on and doors locked for the evening. This is when Townley comes alive with things from the other side.

In 1984 there was a spate of alarms going off at the Hall in the middle of the night. The police arrived with a member of staff to turn the alarm off one cold, dark night in November of that year. All the rooms were checked, and one officer ran up the twisting staircase to the long gallery. Just as he entered the gallery, he heard the sound of a spinet playing, the music was coming from one of the many rooms on the long gallery. Suddenly the music stopped, he instantly turned, and as he glanced to his right, he saw two persons in period dress.

The policeman's first reaction was, "What's going on? The building is locked!"

One of the two characters was a male, giving the appearance of Lord Percy on Black Adder, bowed and grabbing the hand of his female partner simply vanished in to thin air. Of course no one believed the constable, but as he was given a cup of sweet tea to calm him down in the hall's kitchen, he noticed a set of paperback books about the Hall's history. He skipped through the pages, and his jaw dropped as he looked at the portrait of Colonel Francis Townley. He knew who it was that he had seen, even if his colleagues did not believe him.

Townley Hall is well worth a visit.

Chapter 16
Highway Robbery in the Ribble Valley

The Three Fishes public house is situated on the old Yorkshire - Lancashire border, built around the 1720s. The Inn gets its name from the three nearby rivers Calder, Hodder and Ribble.

The Inn is extremely popular for meals, its fantastic countryside views across the Ribble Valley and indeed its roomy atmosphere. It is also famous for stories relating to a young man from Colchester in Essex, known as Ned King, who resided there in the 1730s.

King was a wanted man in Essex - he had committed highway robbery with another infamous Essex man, Dick Turpin. Both men had come up north to escape the authorities, and had huge wagers on their heads. They at first stayed at the nearby Punch Bowl Inn, and that's when Turpin spoke to his young friend King about moving on from the area,

"Lets try the city of York, it's very quiet round here. We need some trade." But King actually liked the peaceful West Riding countryside.

"No, Turpin, I will stay here." he said. The following day Turpin set of for York and within a year found himself on the York gallows in 1739. In the meantime King had befriended the Three Fishes landlord John Briscoe, and between them they started their trade in highway robbery. The Inn was two hundred yards from the Mitton crossroads, an ideal place to hold up coaches. Briscoe and King had a huge advantage, as they both had access to the guests that would stay at both the Punch Bowl and Three Fishes Inns. There they would not only note the route the coaches were planning to take but also find out just how much jewellery and cash these people had with them.

King was employed by both Inns as a Groomsman, and he took great delight in organising the highway robberies. He would ride at great speed to the Mitton crossroads, where he would hide behind the hedgerow and as the coach made its way to the crossroads, shout those famous words, "stand and deliver." The crossroads were ideal for this work as the routes was extremely important for travellers. To the east was Lancaster, to the west Manchester, to the north was Yorkshire and to the south Preston and London.

Between them King and Briscoe held up at least 14 coaches from 1739 -1741, netting a small fortune. But all good things come to an end. When the authorities made attempts to capture them, in those days the police did not exist, but the red coats did and a platoon were sent to capture or indeed kill them. The captain in charge of the section got twelve of his best marksmen in a bogus coach and the plan was to kill the highwaymen by pretending to be civilians. On a beautiful May evening, the coach left Whalley to make its way to Preston. Behind the hedgerow Ned King waited, with both pistols cocked and ready. He heard the sound of horses and the coach made its way to the crossroads. Ned King's heart raced and his mouth went dry as it always did on these occasions. He maneuvered in to the middle of the crossroads and as the coach slowed down, its driver pretended to look shocked.

King shouted "Stand and Deliver!" Suddenly twelve muskets protruded out of the coach window, and the order 'Fire!' was given. King felt intense pain, as two musket balls entered his chest. Luckily he was sitting on his white mare at the time, and although in great pain he galloped at great speed back to the Three Fishes.

On getting to the Inn, he shouted to Briscoe. "The army is hot on my tail!" Both men had a contingency plan for this situation. They had loaded muskets in the attic of the Inn, and both men took up firing positions.

King was bleeding very badly, one of his lungs had been punctured from the ammunition that had hit him. They opened the attic window. This gave them a full view of the road leading from the Mitton crossroads. The army platoon advanced towards the inn and took up firing positions, completely surrounding the Three Fishes Inn.

The platoon's captain shouted, from his hidden position, "You are surrounded! I order you to come out."

Ned King shouted "Never!" and responded by firing in the direction of the voice. Musket balls ricocheted on the walls of the Inn as the army volley fired.

King shouted to Briscoe, "You make a run for it mate, I am done for," looking down at his blood soaked shirt.

Briscoe made his way to the attic window and climbed on to the roof. He ran along the length of the roof of the Inn, and then down the ivy covered wall, all the time - by some miracle, avoiding being hit. Briscoe ran across the fields at the back of the Three Fishes. A trooper carefully aimed and fired, hitting Briscoe cleanly in his back. Within moments Briscoe was surrounded and another trooper delivered another shot this time to his head, killing him instantly.

In the meantime Kings blood loss made him very weak and he fired his last round at the red coats. After a delay in firing, the Captain assumed that King had no ammunition left and entered the inn. He ran upstairs with four men. And there in the corner of the attic was indeed Ned King, slowly bleeding to death.

The Captain grabbed him by the shirt collar, "Right my friend, it was my duty to take you to Preston to face trial for highway robbery, but you have killed three of my best men, so I am going to hang you before you die."

King was pushed down the attic stairs, and then two troopers threw a rope over the nearest oak tree outside the inn, then quickly made a noose to dispatch the highway robber to the next world. King was so weak he did not put up any resistance, and soon found himself hoisted from his feet. Eventually, after Ned King's feet stopped twitching, the army dug a grave by the crossroads and King's warm body was thrown without dignity in to the freshly dug shallow grave.

Well, over the years Ned's ghost has been seen on many occasions. One of the most famous sightings took place during the long, hot summer of 1976, near the Mitton crossroads.

Not far from the place that Ned King once held up all those travellers is a farm. The farmer was horrified one day to watch his barn catch fire. He immediately telephoned the Fire Brigade. Clitheroe station dispatched a crew, and when they got there some ten minutes after the alarm was raised the crew realised that this was indeed a huge fire. They needed help, by means of another engine. A tender was dispatched from Blackburn, at great speed.

As the Blackburn crews advanced towards the Mitton crossroads, the driver shouted, "Bloke on a horse!" He tried to swerve to miss the white mare and its rider, but, in total horror the fire engine ran him over. The crew broke every rule in the fire brigade's training manual by stopping a fire engine on its way to a fire.

Four crew members jumped out of the vehicle and the driver reversed. The entire crew were very surprised and indeed puzzled by the absence of any horse or rider.

"There's nothing there lads. I swear I saw this bloke on a horse!" insisted the brigade driver. Well they were late for the fire, and on getting back to Blackburn each member of the crew had to make a full statement in to the incident.

They all confirmed that the fire engine had indeed run a horse and its rider over. In the autumn of 2003 taxi driver Mark Pinder was driving back from the town of Longridge towards Clitheroe. As he made his way to the crossroads his headlights illuminated a figure some forty yards in front of him. As he swerved to miss the rider, the horse turned and jumped right over his cab, and into the field near the Three Fishes Inn.

Both of these incidents have gone down in local folk law as ghostly encounters of Ned King, the Ribble

Valley highwayman. If you make your way to the city of York, and the City Mews Museum, you can enter the famous cell, known as the "condemned cell." It's here that Turpin spent his last night on this earth.

Through modern technology a hologram of Turpin will appear telling the story of how he and King left Essex and how both men found themselves on the end of a rope.

Chapter 17
The Golden Fleece in the City of York

The city of York is one of the United Kingdom's most haunted cities. Just off a street called "Whipmawhopmagate," is a very famous inn called "The Fleece." And like most of York's public houses, this place has a very famous ghostly story relating to it.

During World War 2, RAF Lynton-on-Ouse was one of Bomber Commands largest bomber bases. The base had units from all across the commonwealth.

The bomber crews faced death every mission and the attrition losses were huge, not many crews completed thirty tours. The average age of these aircrews was twenty one.

If operations were scrubbed, these boys would make their way to the city of York for some very serious alcohol abuse, as a way of dealing with stress and strain. To this day in Betty's tea rooms, you will see a unique mirror downstairs. It's very hard to see your face because many an aircrew member has scratched his initials on to the mirror by using the diamonds in their rings. This is a very sad mirror as the vast majority of the names scratched onto it lost their lives on operations. An expert on RAF bomber command located a number of Victoria Cross recipients' names on the mirror. This famous mirror proudly serves as a monument to them and their supreme sacrifice.

One bitterly cold January morning during the second World War, flying on one engine, Wellington Z for Zulu crossed the Dutch coast. She had two dead on board and by some miracle had flown from Hannover and had not only been damaged by ack ack but harried by night fighters on the journey back. The crew were all Canadian and were on their fourteenth operation. They all knew that they would be extremely lucky to get back, due to the Wellington's appalling damage.

The navigator shouted down his headset mike, "Skipper that's the north sea next stop England."

The skipper answered back, "We are losing fuel and height!"

In the rear Turret sat 20 year old Neil McArdy from Ottawa. He had opened fire on searchlights over Hannover in an attempt to put them out, and was low on ammunition. He hoped and prayed that the German night fighter would not attack again. He was certainly more fortunate than his best pal Eddie from British Columbia - the front gunner who minutes earlier had been killed by a lurking night fighter.

The Wellington was rapidly approaching the Lincolnshire coast, much to the relief of the Skipper. Neil was practically imprisoned in the rear turret, he was also frozen - due to the damage to his turret. The night fighter had shot away some of the Perspex and frozen night air was literally freezing him to death. He had been flying for the past seven hours. He glanced at his watch which read 5.35 am.

"Nearly home," he muttered hopefully through chattering teeth.

At that moment he heard a startling announcement in his ear phones. "Fighter Corkscrew starboard!"

The Wellington, flying on its remaining engine banked left, and the Messhersmidt 110 opened fire, sending tracer in to the stricken plane, killing the navigator and flight engineer and wounding the pilot.

Neil felt the plane lurch badly, he heard a voice - it was the skipper. In a desperately distressed voice he pleaded, "Ok Guys! Abandon ship!"

There was no power in the Turret, to turn it round for Neil to make his escape. It was the stuff of your very worst nightmare. Neil was physically trapped in this flying coffin. He again heard the words from the Skipper, "Jump guys!"

Neil placed his mask around his mouth.

"Skipper, I am trapped!" he screamed.

"Okay. My legs have had it, I cannot get out either," said the Skipper. "I will do my best to get her on to land."

As it happened, Neil and the Skipper were the only two left alive out of all the crew. They had trained together, and now it seemed they would die together.

By some miracle, the Me 110 had broken off the engagement. The Wellington's amazing canvas and wood structure had somehow held together. The Skipper had a broken leg and wounds in both his head and left arm. Lynton-on-Ouse airbases' flare path was lit. The Wellington had no way of contacting base as the radio communications transmission equipment had been shot away in the battle. The bomber had no wheels and the skipper in terrible pain from his wounds.

Despite all of the odds stacked against the perished aircraft, the Skipper somehow levelled the bomber and skillfully belly landed the Wellington Z, in a mass of sparks and flames. The RAF fire crews raced at great speed to the burning bomber.

Neil felt the heat down the length of the fuselage, and thought, "I have got back from Hannover, just to be burned alive on a Yorkshire field." He looked up through the bullet ridden Perspex canopy of the turret, "So this is the end of my life. Completely trapped inside my tiny compartment."

Suddenly he heard voices and the sound of smashing Perspex and the cutting of metal. The crash crews had reached him. He was carefully lifted out of the rear turret.

"Are you okay pal?" said a member of the rescue team.

"Yeah, thanks." said Neil. "I am just frozen stiff!"

He was helped in to the back of a crew vehicle and for the first time in 8 hours his limbs had access to full blood supply. The relief on his face was unmistakable. He looked out of the back of the vehicle and could still see the blazing wreck of the Wellington on the runway.

"Are my buddies okay?" he asked.

The reply cut through him. "Sorry pal. They are all dead."

Neil swallowed hard. "Those guys were like family to me. How the hell can this happen?"

He was taken to dispersal, and interviewed about the raid. He was deeply saddened by the cold lack of feeling the interviewing officer had with regards the death of his crew mates.

"All right, McArdy. I am transferring you to a new crew." he said in a cold, unsympathetic voice.

Neil walked back to his billet, and sat on his bed. He gazed down the length of the Nissan hut, and sighed deeply as he looked at the four empty beds that only 20 hours ago his buddies had all woken up in. He lit a cigarette, and he heard a voice inside his head.

"It's only a matter of time before you join them Neil." He knew he was going to die, it could be tonight or next week or next month. But one thing Neil was certain of was that he was due to die.

"You are bound to get the chop soon," said the voice in his head. He had breakfast and to his great relief was informed that ops had been cancelled for tonight, due to low cloud over the Ruhr Valley. He had a shave, put his best uniform on and made his way to the guard room for a pass.

He caught the local bus in to the City of York. The bus made its way over Lendal Bridge, and the River Ouse.

"What a beautiful city," he whispered to himself. It was a dry day if a little cold. Neil was on a mission, which was to consume as much alcohol as was humanely possible. His first stop, the "Old Starre Inn" on Stonegate. He made his way into the bar.

"Yes lad?" said the landlord.

"A pint please and a whiskey chaser."

"Okay lad but there is a restriction on whiskey due to rationing."

Neil consumed both drinks in a matter of minutes, left and made his way to Betty's Bar, where he ordered and consumed the same again. He had another hour to go before the 3.00pm closing time. By the time 3.00pm came, Neil was severely inebriated. He was in the snug in the Golden Fleece. The Landlady felt sorry for the young Canadian air gunner.

She said, "Don't worry lad, we have a lock in for you air force types in the bar upstairs. The cops never visit us and you lads deserve a good break from your duties."

The landlady, Vivien, had seen many young boys in exactly the same situation; Canadians, Australians and New Zealanders, many miles from home. And she was well aware just how many of them never came back from operations. She brought up a bottle of whiskey from the bar. Neil was joined by an Australian Navigator and a fellow Canadian gunner. It turned out that these two had been on a similar mission.

The Navigator, in a highly inebriated voice, informed both of his drinking partners, "Well I am on my third crew, my luck has got to run out soon. All my mates are dead, they keep transferring me to a new crew. I will be honest with you lads, I am scared shitless. I have a wife and kid back in Melbourne. They won't see me again."

Neil took all this in, knowing that he was in exactly the same predicament. He filled his glass, "Well guys, here's to us." The three of them stood up and had a toast. Within minutes the bottle was empty. Vivien was aware that these boys were practically paralytic, but she felt for them, and had a great respect for them. Although spirits were rationed, she found another bottle.

"I must have a leak," said Neil. The room spun round with every step, trying to go forward seemed to make him walk backwards. The upstairs toilet faced the top of the stairs. Neil got to the toilet door and in a jerking motion,

123

pulled the door open with force. Suddenly the effect of the alcohol got to him and he fell backwards and down the stairs violently. On the way down he spun round and fell awkwardly accidentally breaking his neck. His body fell grotesquely on the base of the staircase, his eyes open staring in to space. Yes, as he had morbidly forecast, Neil had died on operations. But not in the way that he anticipated.

His two drinking partners staggered down the stairs to pick him up. The Aussie navigator stammered, "The poor lad's bought it, would you bloody believe it," he muttered.

Neil's squadron where informed of his sad death, and by strange coincidence the crew he had been transferred to at the aerodrome were all killed the following night.

If you go to Betties Bar in York today, have a look at the mirror and all those names. And consider yourself very lucky that your generation does not have to go through what these young men had to. Today the Golden Fleece in the city of York has a reputation for being one of the most haunted public houses in the city.

In 1975 William and Jane Edmondson from Ottawa booked in to the Golden Fleece for bed and breakfast. They enjoyed a full day sightseeing and then an evening meal followed by a few drinks in the bar, before retiring upstairs to bed.

They both fell in to a deep sleep. William suddenly heard a soft voice, coming within the room.

The voice had an unmistakable Canadian accent. "Hey Buddy, oh it's so good to hear someone from home!"

William thought "What's this guy doing in our bedroom? I locked the door." He jumped out of bed and put the light on. Apart from his sleeping wife there was nobody else in the room.

The following Morning he told his wife. She laughed, "You're hearing things!" she said, over the breakfast table.

However, another person overheard the conversation. "Excuse me," said seventy five year old Vivien - The ex landlady. Her Granddaughter was the landlady now, and she helped her Granddaughter run the hotel now.

"The Golden Fleece was very popular with Canadian air force personel during World War 2. A lot of brave boys drank here before operations."

She went on to mention Sergeant Neil McArdy from Ottawa, and how the poor lad had drunk himself to death and indeed fallen down the stairs.

"We are from Ottawa also." They had just one more night to stay in York, before heading north to their next destination, Edinburgh. So, an early night was planned. The Edmondsons closed the curtains, locked the bedroom door and got into bed.

William heard a whisper again, "Hey buddy, I have been here since 1942, I want to go home."

William felt no fear and asked for a name.

"Sergeant Neil McArdy," was the reply.

"Look son, I believe you but I am not a medium or psychic. What the hell can I do?"

The soft Canadian voice whispered back, "You're Canadians from my home town Ottawa. Please could you get some help. I am trapped in space in this room, I want to go home. Please help me."

William sighed deeply, surprisingly he was not frightened, perhaps it was the soft Canadian voice, and being a fellow compatriot, he felt he would have to help.

"What can I do?" he whispered back, for fear of waking his wife.

"Bring a priest back home from Ottawa. Also can you please see if my name is on the Ottawa City War Memorial?"

William whispered back, "Son, is there any chance I can look at you, do you have a face?"

"You may see me, in the reflection of the mirror in

the bathroom."

"Okay son." William made his way to the bathroom, and turned the light on.

"Are you there son?" asked William.

"I am right behind you." William gazed at the bathroom mirror and slowly but surely, a handsome, well manicured young man's face transpired in the mirror, wearing a Canadian air force battledress top. Again, for some strange reason William was not scared, but filled with deep sympathy.

"How old are you son?"

"Well, I was twenty years old when I lost my life here in 1942. I just cannot get away from this room. I have tried but keep hitting a blank wall. I know I have to go to the next world but cannot escape this living death. Please help me."

William looked in to the Mirror. "Son, I promise I will do all I can for you."

Surprisingly when his wife woke up the following morning, he didn't tell her of this ghostly encounter. But on getting back home to Ottawa, he contacted the Royal Canadian Air Force to look at their military records on air crews in World War Two and was actually horrified at just how many young Canadian boys had lost their lives on bombing raids on Nazi Germany.

William then made his way to the RCAF memorial in the city and again was deeply touched by the sheer amount of countless names. He glanced down alphabetically. "Sergeant Neil McArdy aged 20," came in to view.

William whispered to himself, "I am going to bring you home son."

He had given a lot of thought and consideration to the words that he had heard in the Fleece, but wondered how he might convince a priest, or indeed anyone that what he had seen that day was indeed the ghost of a Canadian airman.

He visited the city Cathedral, and had an interview with a member of the cathedral authorities. He was told, "Sorry, we do not get involved with paranormal investigations," and he was politely asked to leave.

William felt very deflated, and walked through the city centre, past a news stand. There he glanced at a collection of magazines and one seemed to catch his eye. The magazine was called "Paranormal Monthly". He skipped through the pages and noticed an advert.

"Have you got a story of a paranormal nature? Can our team exercise your home and free its tortured spirits?" William reached in to his pocket for some cash and purchased the magazine. On getting home he looked at the advert again, and decided to telephone the number. It was a Montreal number and the lady that answered had a very strong French-Canadian accent.

"Please could you help me," said William.

"Sure. Fire away," came the answer. William had an attentive listener and told the woman on the end of the line all about his experience in York with the Canadian air gunner.

"Well, that is quite some experience!" said Adele Petain. She informed William that she was a psychic and his story had fascinated her.

"I must come and see you," she said in an excited voice. Two days later he heard a knock on the door. On his step stood a very attractive young woman with blonde hair, red lipstick and cutting the curves of Marilyn Monroe.

"Come in," said William. "Well, thank you for coming so far to see me."

"Your story has fascinated me Mr Edmondson, I really want to help."

William made his visitor a coffee and they sat down to talk.

"I suggest we go to York and free this young man's spirit."

"How can you help?"

"Well I can see into the past. I am a medium, and I have been in situations like this before. It seems that the day after Sergeant McArdy died, the rest of his Squadron were killed in the skies over Dusseldorf. He seems to have cheated his destiny, by losing his life in The Fleece the night before. It seems that the spirit world had him booked in to the next world, the day after but he did not turn up with the rest of his crew as scheduled - because of his drunken death in the pub. Sometimes even the spirit world can make mistakes." she said, fascinating William with all that Adele had learnt.

"We must go to England, this Saturday. Don't worry about the cost, my magazine will pay for the flights and the accommodation in York."

William was thrilled, he couldn't believe that he had actually managed to find somebody that could help him keep the promise he made to the figure in the mirror.

"How can I explain this to my wife, Jane?" he asked. "My wife knows nothing of my ghostly encounter."

"Well, we can both tell her."

You can only imagine how William's wife Jane felt when she heard the story and, the thought of her husband jetting of to England with a beautiful young woman. For a few seconds she got the impression that she was being taken for a ride. But Jane had known William for the past 30 years and could always tell when he was being honest. With a sigh she agreed that he should go with this blonde haired beauty to England. William was old enough to be her father, she reasoned.

Two days later, they were on an Air Canada flight to Newcastle. Adele had contacted the Golden Fleece and informed the Landlady about their impending visit and asked for permission to conduct an exorcism in the room where William and Jane had stayed.

On Arriving in York, Adele's words were, "Wow, just look at this place. I love it." She took inthe elegant shape of the mighty York Minster, admired Skeldergate

Bridge and was fascinated by The Shambles.

Eventually, they made their way to The Fleece. Waiting on their arrival at the door was Vivien, the ex landlady. "Welcome," she said. "Please come this way. Nice to see you again Mr Edmondson."

"Thank you. This visit does mean a lot to me," he said.

Adele entered the building and made her way to the bar. Two boys at the bar turned round as she made her way in. Adele instantly knew she was the subject of attraction, she was used to it. Vivien and William followed in to the bar.

"Right, I will take you to your rooms." said Vivien.

They made their way upstairs. Adele stopped at the top of the stairs.

"This is where Neil Fell in 1942," said Adele.

"That's right." said a startled Vivien. "You are quite right."

"Yes, I can feel a real presence already," said Adele.

"When do you want to start your exorcism?" asked William.

"Well it's your bedroom we need to conduct our work in," she replied.

They had a meal and then with Vivien's help, cordoned off the top flight of stairs. Adele asked that all the lights be turned off. She opened her suitcase and took out three candle holders and placed a candle in each holder and lit all three of the candles. It felt very calm and very quiet upstairs, and the light from the candles gave an eerie glow across the landing facing all three of the upstairs bedrooms.

"Okay, it's time to start." said Adele. She sat at the top of the stairs where Neil had fallen all those years ago.

"Neil, make your presence felt." said Adele, with her eyes closed.

A breeze came across the landing, and William felt

something behind him.

"Thanks Buddy. Have you come to take me home?" the familiar voice said.

Vivien screamed. "It's him!" she shouted.

"Shush! Be quiet!" demanded Adele.

"Okay Hun."

"We are here to take you back to Ottawa," said Adele.

"Could you show yourself in the mirror in the room again?" asked William.

Adele, William and Vivien made their way in to the bedroom, and looked at the mirror. There in solid form, looking out of the mirror was Sergeant Neil McArdy.

"Please folks I want to go home."

"Neil, we are here to help you get home, I have the means, but you are going to have to do exactly what I tell you," said Adele, as she ushered Vivien and William to the top of the stairs.

She grabbed their hands and said, "We must embrace each other as one. Neil, you must come in to the middle of all three of us and we must give you our body warmth for you to exit this room and enter the next world."

After a few seconds Adele looked happy.

"He is right in-between us!"

William was not scared but felt a huge cold blast on his chest. Vivien, who was a rather plump woman also felt the huge temperature drop.

"Neil with our warmth, make your way up and out of this prison."

William glanced to his left and noticed the door to the bedroom with the mirror was ajar and then suddenly open fully. He could clearly see Neil's ghost in the centre of the three of them, almost feeding off their body warmth.

Then, they heard a word of pure joy in a strong Canadian accent.

"Oh God, thank you I am free."

The ghostly figure in the mirror surrounded by the

three suddenly vaporised and disappeared.

"He has entered the other world!" announced a jubilant Adele. "He is with his Canadian relatives." Tears spilled down William and Vivien's faces.

"That poor lad has been here for over 30 years. I have never forgotten that day he died, or any of his brave mates." said Vivien.

Adele said with a huge smile on her face, "Well guys, let's have a drink to celebrate this young man's freedom."

William was not a drinker, but today he felt like celebrating.

"Let's paint the town Canadian red!" he said happily. The trio of jubilant people went down to the bar, and drink followed more drink. William was feeling the effect of the whiskey,

"I am just going for a leak," he said as he staggered away from the table, to use the loo at the top of the stairs. As he got to the top step he staggered back, lost his footing and fell backwards at speed falling awkwardly. Just like Sergeant Neil McArdy had done, William sadly broke his neck.

Vivien and Adele came rushing out of the bar as a result of the noise, and found Williams warm dead body at the base of the stairs.

Adele instantly looked to her right in to the landing mirror. There looking in a deep distressed state was William Edmondson's ghostly face starring out of the mirror.

Chapter 18
THE CURSE OF ALICE NUTTER

If you make your way to the village of Roughlee, situated in the shadow of one of Great Britain's most famous hills, Pendle Hill, you will come across a statue of a very famous local woman known as Alice Nutter.

Her statue has her back to the city of Lancaster and is in chains. Alice was executed in the City of Lancaster on the 20th of August 1612. Alice was executed for the crime of witchcraft.

In East Lancashire there are some 50,000 Pendle Witch experts, and all those experts seem to have a different outlook on the trials. The only window we have in to the event, is a book written by Mr Thomas Potts Clerk to the courts in Lancaster at the 1612 trials. This book is called "the wonderful discovery of witches in Lancashire" published in 1613. We have to believe that his book is honest and indeed accurate. By far the most interesting character in the trial seems to be Alice Nutter.

Many Historians seem to have gained a huge amount of respect for her as she does come across in Potts book as being an exceptionally brave woman. In the year 1612 women had no rights whatsoever, and were considered to be incapable of actually using a brain, or indeed possessing one. Alice, it seems, was an intelligent woman. She found herself in an era that was very dangerous for ladies of her intellect.

Let's turn the clock back in time to those rather sad days. One thing that has not changed is man's determination to make himself look good in the eyes of his superiors. One such man that Thomas Potts book does bring to light is local Magistrate Roger Nowell. None of us were alive in 1612, but one does get the impression that this man was on a mission to curry favour with King James the 1st. It was said that the king was convinced that witches not only existed but were actually out to get him. As a result he wrote a book called the demonology book, and this book was used as a guide to not only try witches but also given to magistrates across the country.

East Lancashire was a predominately Catholic area at this time, with wealthy Catholic landowners at Samlesbury hall, Townley Hall and Stoney Hurst. So the king did view the area with a degree of distrust.

Living beneath the shadow of Pendle Hill in 1612 were persons who like you and I had to eat and had to find clothing and also shelter. Some of these people could only be described as peasants with very low levels of education, if any at all.

But you have to have income, to survive, and the best form of income would be to beg or in some cases make some form of herbal remedy for sale to the public. The impression I personally get from reading Potts book is that these so called witches were indeed a nuisance to travellers and persons and their begging and bother making must have reached the ears of the local magistrate Nowell. I believe this man was on a mission.

Our story starts on the 18th of March when a young woman called Alison Devize had the misfortune of meeting a Halifax peddler called John Law. She had no money and just begged for pins off him. He refused and became agitated and collapsed, and found to his horror he had become paralysed down the left side of his body. Very likely the effects of a stroke.

In court later that year he informed the court that Alison had a dog with her that talked. This action was reported to the Magistrate. Alison was arrested along with her Grandmother, Elisabeth Southern, Anne Whittle and her daughter Anne Redfearne. They were all sent to the city of Lancaster and chained to the floor in appalling conditions.

Nowell was elated, "If I can incriminate these persons the King will be very impressed!" He thought.

A short while later at the home of Alison Devize, a

stone cottage called Malkin Tower, a meeting took place on Good Friday. The idea was to blow the gates of Lancaster castle open and free their loved ones. According to Potts book, word of this meeting reached the ears of Nowell and he insisted that these persons should be arrested.

On hearing of this impending arrest some people that had been in attendance of the meeting had the good sense not to wait around to be arrested and find themselves on the end of a rope. Those that were successfully captured and imprisoned at Lancaster and York were Jennet Preston, Elizabeth Devize, her son and daughter Alison and James as well as Katherine Hewitt along with Alice Grey. Others seized were John and Jane Bulcock, Margaret Pearson and our heroin Alice Nutter.

The King heard about the arrests and had two circuit judges sent to Lancaster Castle, along with Nowell and two more magistrates Bannister and Holden. Thomas Potts clerk was also there, his job was to make a complete report on the trial. As I mentioned, his book was published 400 years ago and it is the only window we have. I personally think that these so called witches, had evidence against them fabricated, and I believe that Magistrate Nowell was the main instigator of this. Remember this man wanted to curry favour with King James.

None of us will ever know how these people were treated in the dungeon at Lancaster, though we understand that Elizabeth Southern (alias Demdyke) died before the trials began, most likely as a result of the treatment that was meted out to her. Some of the accusations against them consisted of making clay pictures of their victims, also possessing dogs that could change in to human beings, and hares that could spit flames.

Jennet Preston was executed in York in July of that year. Her crime was to be at the so called Good Friday meeting and also for the murder of her employer Thomas Lister, by witchcraft. She had nursed him, and when he died wrapped his body in a clean white sheet, ready for burial. Some fresh blood came through the sheeting, andthis was classed as witchcraft. At her trial in York, her husband came with her and indeed villagers to beg for her release. But the Prosecution had found her guilty before she had even stepped foot in the court. Nowell must have been looking forward very much to the trials. When the trials began at Lancaster the accused had no defence whatsoever.

Demdyke in her absence was found guilty of the deaths by witchcraft of Richard Assheton, Henry Mitton and the baby daughter of Richard Baldwin.

Old Chattox was found guilty of the murders of Robert Nutter, John Devize, Anne Nutter, John Moore and Hugh Moore.

Katherine Hewitt was found guilty for the murder of Anne Foulds.

Elizabeth Devize was found guilty of the murders of John Robinson, James Robinson, Henry Mitton, James Devize, Anne Townley, John Hargreaves, Blaze Hargreaves, John Duckworth, Anne Redfearne and Christopher Nutter.

Nowell must have felt elated. He did have his trump card up his sleeve; he had kept the youngest of the Devize Children with him at his home, Read Hall. For the first time in her life she had three warm meals a day, nice clothes to wear and her own bed. After this grooming she was only too happy to incriminate her entire family, and that's exactly what she did. Nowell took her to the courts in the castle and placed her on a table so the jury could see her.

Once there she shouted to the jury, "My grandmother, mother, brother and sister are all witches. I have seen them curse people.

Her mother shouted, "Stop it! You don't know what you are saying."

At this point Jeanette asked the court to remove her mother as she was upsetting her. Her mother was indeed taken back to the cells. Nowell's plan was working perfectly, these past few months he had got confessions from the defendants who, also due to being scared stiff, had tried to blame others, in the hope that they would be freed.

You may be wondering if these people had been tortured. Well in Potts book it mentions the case of James Devize. He had to be carried in to the court by two warders his health was in a terrible state. And Potts wondered if he had indeed been tortured.

Standing in the dock that day was Alice Nutter. She had seen the torture downstairs in the cells, and watched Demdyke actually being kicked to death as she had refused to admit to witchcraft. Alice's health was also in a serious state. She had refused to sign a confession and as a result Nowell had her put on a starvation diet. Alice's problems had started some months previously. She was a reasonably wealthy woman and had owned land, her husband was a successful farmer. On occasions some of her neighbours would take land without permission. Alice asked her husband to get the land disputes sorted in court. He was too scared, so she had to go by herself.

Despite knowing that, as a woman, she was breaking the law, she barged in to the courts in Clitheroe and Lancaster and demanded that her land disputes were dealt with. Well, she won every case, but in doing so she did embarrass Roger Nowell to such a degree that he was determined to get rid of her as a thorn in his side along with two other farmers, John and Jane Bulcock. Like Alice, they had also complained about their land disputes and as a result they too had to be eradicated. And what an excellent cover up - if they could be found guilty of witchcraft their nuisance value would be terminated.

Nowell was delighted when young Jeanette Devize pointed out on his direction the defendants Alice Nutter, John and Jane Bulcock as being at the Good Friday meeting at Malkin tower. John and his mother Jane were both mortified when found guilty of turning a young girl completely mad, and naturally they pleaded their innocence. A cruel smile came across Nowell's face as Alice Nutter, although in a state of severe starvation, elegantly made her way to the centre of the court and was found guilty of the murder of Henry Mitton, as he would not give her, Demdyke or Alison Devize a penny.

Alice knew that she had indeed been, to use a modern term, 'Stitched up'. It was obvious that she did not need to beg and she had never come across Alison Devize or indeed her grandmother. But nevertheless, she was found guilty. She had made a plea of not guilty, but she knew this plea would go unheard.

The Pendle Witches were then made to walk to the pillory, a short walk from Lancaster castle. We can only imagine the horror they must have gone through on their short journey to the gallows.

The group stopped and then had to mount the pillory where they stood on stools. A huge crowd came to watch this rather cruel death. They had their hands tied behind their backs, and then the nooses placed around their necks. Their body weight would actually kill them there was no drop.

Alice bravely turned to watch this huge crowd gather to watch their deaths. Suddenly in this crowd she noticed Magistrate Roger Nowell, she caught his eye and shouted from the gallows, "I shall haunt you for the rest of your life!"

Then the stools were kicked away and they began to strangle to death turning purple in the face, a very slow, painful and traumatic death.

Nowell, with a cruel smile on his face, was elated, his mission was completed. He felt a child's hand try to hold his own. It was his trump card, nine year old Jeanette who had just witnessed the cold bloodied murder of her mother, brother and sister.

"Are we going home now Uncle Roger?" she asked with a smile on her face.

Nowell looked down at the girl, and cruelly slapped her across the face and said, "Goodbye, you have served your purpose!" Jeanette with tears in her eyes pleaded to be taken back to Read Hall and all its comforts.

"Get out of my sight." he shouted.

Jeanette made a rather pathetic figure as she walked over the Trough of Bowland, back to Pendle and the old empty stone cottage, Malkin Tower. On entering the cold ruin she took in the tragedy, that she had indeed been used by Nowell as his pawn to make him look good in the courts.

We do know that many years later Jeanette was arrested and taken back to Lancaster, on a charge of witchcraft. You could say Witchcraft had ruined this woman's life and also destroyed her family. Magistrate Roger Nowell sent a message down to King James, to inform him he had just dispatched 10 witches. He was immediately made High Sheriff of Lancashire with a huge increase in salary. He had indeed curried favour with the king. Thomas Potts had no idea at the time but his book the wonderful discovery also earned him a lot of money.

Nowell made his way back to the Hall, extremely satisfied with himself. "Well the beggars have all gone on the hill, I shall have no more complaints from travellers from now on. And those troublesome farmers, with their pathetic land disputes."

He poured himself a large glass and celebrated the success of the day. He then got into bed but found sleep impossible. He kept seeing this image of Alice Nutter on the gallows,

"I shall haunt you!" The words kept echoing in his head. He tossed and turned in bed, Alice's image literally haunting him.

Before he knew it, daylight appeared through the curtains, "I have not slept. That damn woman has been in my head all night."

He got out of bed and shouted for his servant to make breakfast. "A good walk will do me good," he said, "Exercise is what I need."

He consumed his breakfast and walked from Read Hall in to the village of Whalley, where he made his way to the old ruins of Whalley Abbey by the banks of the River Calder.

"This fresh air will do me good," he said. "And after I have walked back to Reed Hall, a good sleep will restore my health." He stopped by the river bank and gazed in to the water for a few seconds, the river was quite deep at this section, very calm and mirror flat. He could clearly see his reflection in the water.

Suddenly at great speed another reflection came, gazing out of the water at him. He watched with curiosity as the reflection materialised. It was Alice Nutter, her finger was pointing at him, just as she had from the gallows. Nowell heard a voice in his head, "I will haunt you for the rest of your life." Screaming in terror, he ran in the direction of Whalley,

"Oh My God, she is haunting me!" he said to himself.

He walked at great speed back to Reed Hall along the narrow lanes that had once been used by Demdyke and her granddaughter Alison Devize to beg off travellers. He felt the hedgerows were all alive with eyes watching his every move, the slightest rustle from the trees induced a fear in him.

At last his home was in view, he rushed inside, "I need alcohol," he said. "I will sleep after I have had some sustenance." He ordered his servant to have a warm meal made and his bed chamber also prepared.

The fact that Nowell had not slept in 36 hours and the warm meal and alcohol had taken effect, as soon as he placed his head on the pillow, he began to drift in to a warm comfortable sleep.

"To hell with Alice Nutter!" he whispered to himself, "she caused me a lot of concern from members of my community, she was always complaining about her land being taken. Well where she has gone there will be plenty of room!" he sniggered after the effects of drink."

Outside the weather elements had changed dramatically. A strong wind blew and with it very heavy rain began to batter on his bedroom window. It was late August, so his window was slightly ajar, and a gust of wind blew the window fully open. This caused his bed curtains to flutter, blow and sway around. Heavy thunder and lightening was illuminating the sky, the thunder was so loud it woke the Magistrate, from a deep sleep.

"Oh," he sighed "I had better close the window."

In a state of semi sleep he pulled the bed clothes to his side and got out of his four poster, and walked to the open window. The wooden floor boards creaked beneath him as he walked. He slammed the window shut, and secured the catch. He then turned to walk back to his bed. Nowell's eyes widened in pure shock as he looked towards his bed. There he could make out the silhouettes of three people standing still by his bed.

A flash of lightening illuminated the room.

"Oh Jesus help me!" The magistrate shouted. The room darkened again but, was again illuminated by yet another lightening bolt. He could clearly see the figures of Demdyke and Alison Devize. The third figure was Alice Nutter. He ran for the door to escape the ghosts. As he opened the door to run down the twisting staircase, there at the end of the landing stood two more figures. A flash of lightening brought them both into the light. Nowell instantly recognised them as John and Jane Bulcock.

Nowell screamed again, in pure terror. He ran down the stairs and out into the open. A voice in his head said 'just keep running.'

"I must get away," he said, "far from here and these damn demons."

Night turned into day, and he took stock of the situation. He was in his nightclothes, soaking to the bone. He had literally covered some 15 miles in the night. He sat on a large stone overlooking the village of Newton in Bowland, wet through and extremely traumatised.

The Horror of what he had taken in was just beginning to sink in. "Yes, I am being haunted, I must get far from here," he muttered.

In a bedraggled and shattered state he walked into Slaidburn village, and made his way into the Bounty Inn.

The Landlord laughed at Nowell's attire and said, "Well sir you look in a very frail state."

"Please could you help me, I am a very wealthy man? Could you please send someone to my home, Read Hall and bring clothes, but also my financial details? I am your magistrate, Roger Nowell," he explained.

"Yes Sir, of Course, I will make sure your wishes are carried out right away Sir."

Nowell made his way to the Inn's fire, sat down in front of it and within seconds sleep had found him. A few hours later he was woken by his servant from Reed Hall, John McIver.

"Mr Nowell, Sir I was very worried about you. I heard you scream last night, I got dressed and searched the house for you, but nothing."

Nowell looked McIver in the eye, "Did you see them?" he shouted with an alarmed look on his face.

"See who Sir?" asked the servant.

"Last night, those witches in the house."

McIver put his hand on Nowell's shoulder in a sympathetic manner.

"Sir, there was no one in the house apart from you and I, that I can confirm Sir."

"I am not going back McIver!" stormed Nowell.

"But Sir, it is your ancestral home!"

"I cannot!" he repeated. "McIver, I am going to have a holiday away from Lancashire. I may go to the Lake District. Please look after the Hall for me and bring me my finances. Thank you McIver."

Nowell spent two more days at the Bounty Inn at Slaidburn, and was very relieved to have no ghostly encounters in his sleep. He then made his way to Kendal, to the delights of the Lake District fells. He stayed at the Hole in the Wall Inn at Bowness. The clean air and the beauty of the area had a good effect on him and eventually, he felt he could put the past behind him and in time return to his native Reed Hall.

One morning, he had breakfast at the inn and dressed for a good walk on the beautiful fells and mountains that surrounded the Inn. He made his way on to Great Gable and then down to Striding Edge. The views took his breath away. He felt so good in himself to be the only person for miles. He had not felt as content for a very long time. The Lake District really had brought the best out of him. He was aware that the King had made him High Sheriff of Lancashire and that he would soon have to return to his duties.

The warm Autumn sun lit up the reflection from the lakes surrounding him, and the autumn leaves created a landscape of red and gold, simply stunning scenery. He got on to the path that would take him on to Striding Edge, a very narrow path, dangerous in winter but passable during the summer months. He happily walked on to the path surrounded by a sheer drop on both sides.

Half way down Striding Edge he looked up into the beautiful blue sky and his attention was caught by the site of a magnificent Golden Eagle. He turned to watch the creatures flight, taking in its fantastic wingspan, the bird seemed to be flying in his direction. As the Eagle flew over him he started to walk backwards, forgetting he was on a narrow path. Suddenly he walked backwards over the edge, and with a scream and flaying arms and legs he fell some 90 feet on to a ledge.

On making contact with the ledge, he felt the air taken from both lungs, and a searing pain stabbed through his insides. Nowell had broken his back, his hip, left arm and both legs. The pain was excruciating. He drifted in and out of consciousness. He could not move due to the seriousness of his injuries. He took stock of his situation.

"I am totally alone. I can not move."

Night soon came but sleep was impossible due to his injuries. At first light he shouted for help, but realised that he was miles from civilisation. A thirst came over him, but he had no access to water. He shouted again, but all he could hear in the distance was the sound of bleating sheep.

Night came again, his thirst had become unbearable and the pain he was in was intolerable as he drifted in and out of consciousness. He became aware of something on his face at first light, and felt a sharp pain in his left eye. With his uninjured right hand he slapped at the side of his face, and pushed a Magpie off his forehead that had tried to remove his eye.

Roger Nowell knew his situation was desperate, and he began to accept the fact that it was highly unlikely that he would be rescued. He was going to die alone on this Lake District mountain. A deep tiredness came over him, his breath became shallow, his view from where he lay took in a larger ledge just above him. As he gazed upwards, he saw a figure pointing down towards him. At first he thought he was about to be rescued. Then he took in some more figures. There were eleven in all, and they all seemed to be laughing at him. "How cruel can this be?" he thought. He glanced again at the figures, and it became clear that the figures he was looking at were the Pendle Witches.

Although in extreme pain, he managed to raise himself up on his right arm. He heard a voice, as Alice Nutter's ghost stood on the ledge next to him. She was pointing in Nowell's face.

"You have taken the lives of twelve innocent people. They are with their maker, but where you are going it is going to get very hot indeed!"

Alice turned to the eleven figures on the ledge above. "Justice has been done!"

As she looked down at Magistrate Roger Nowell's body, she watched as the Angels of Death took him away.

Nowell's ghost shouted, "I am sorry. Please help me, it's the King's fault!" he pleaded. "I beg of you Mistress Nutter to save me."

Alice turned, to the eleven figures dotted around the mountain top.

"Right my friends. Justice has been done."

THE END

© Copyright 2014

By Simon Entwistle

For more information on Simon's ghost walks and tours, visit
www.tophattours.co.uk

Printed in Great Britain
by Amazon